FOREST OF THE DAMNED

LEE MOUNTFORD

For my beautiful wife, Michelle. And amazing daughters, Ella and Sophie.

FREE BOOK

Sign up to my mailing list for a free horror book...

Want more scary stories? Sign up to my mailing list and receive your free copy of *The Nightmare Collection - Vol 1* directly to your email address.

This novel-length short story collection is sure to have you sleeping with the lights on.

Sign up now.

www.leemountford.com

1

JAMES RAISED his glass of dark brown ale. 'I think a toast is in order,' he said, his voice already showing the effects of the alcohol he'd consumed.

Tony smiled, amused at James' inebriated enthusiasm, and he lifted his pint of beer in response. 'And what are we toasting?' Tony asked. Ken and Roberta followed suit with their drinks, raising them up—Ken's a tumbler of amber whiskey and Roberta's a tall glass of red wine. The heat from the fire near to them and the crackle that accompanied the burning of the logs were a nice contrast to the dark skies outside the pub.

Said pub—the Last Lodge—was situated in the small town of Amaley, in Northern Scotland. The bar area of the Lodge was warm and cosy with the large, roaring fire set against an outside wall that was all bare stone, and weathered oak joists supporting low ceilings above. It felt like a traditional, old-world public house, with few patrons in that night excluding Tony's group, who were gathered in a corner booth. A withered old man with a hooked, bright-red nose sat on a stool at the bar opposite the rotund barman and cast them occasional glances as he sipped at his black, foamy pint. A bloodhound lay at the base of the man's stool, curled up and snoring.

'We are toasting us,' James said. His cheeks were rosy and his eyes glassy, but he was in good spirits. His hair, light brown and set in a centre parting over a rather square face, reached down to his eyes, often hiding them when he spoke. He was taller than Tony, at over six foot, but was very thin, even scrawny. 'Or, more specifically, the company,' he continued on and held his glass even higher. 'To Paranormal Encounters Limited. And here's also to having one hell of an investigation. It's going to be a massive success, I just know it.'

Tony noticed that James seemed to be focusing mostly on their leader, Ken, as he spoke, and he had a big smile on his face. A small, rare grin spread beneath Ken's bushy beard in response.

'Very kind of you, James,' Tony said, his voice gruff as usual. 'But it's going to be a long week out there in that forest. And chances are we won't find anything.'

'Nonsense,' James answered with a dismissive wave of his hand. Roberta, who was seated next to him, shook her head, looking slightly embarrassed for her boyfriend and his bold claims. James went on, 'We've picked up some compelling evidence in our recent investigations, but we've only ever had one night to get it. This time, we have a whole week. And what a location! We're going to find something, I'm telling you.'

Of course, Tony hoped James was right. That was the reason they were out here, and the reason Paranormal Encounters existed in the first place. They all had a shared interest in this kind of thing—the paranormal—and it was an interest that was a little too strong to simply call a hobby.

Being from the same area, they had all found each other online, Tony and Ken meeting first five years ago. Tony had already set up his fledgeling company by then, with the sole aim of finding proof of paranormal existence. Between them, they had been on over fifty investigations and had certainly witnessed a few unexplainable things, but what they lacked was anything that could be considered undeniable proof the supernatural existed. After a year, Tony had joined the company officially as a minor shareholder director, but Paranormal Encounters was a company in name only. There was no wage or income to be had—it was merely a front for them to indulge in a pastime they loved, lending themselves some legitimacy in the process. All equipment the company owned had been bought from their own pockets.

A year ago, however, after treading water and doing the same old thing time after time, Tony and Ken met Roberta and James: a younger couple who shared their interest in the paranormal. This young couple were also a lot more tech and media savvy, and showed Ken and Tony ways to push the company into the realms of profitability. Paranormal Encounters suddenly found themselves nicely branded and had a social media presence, all with the aim to piggyback off the success of ghost-hunting TV shows. Their audience, however, was not in front of a TV, but rather online, and the group streamed or uploaded the results of their investigations. Revenue wasn't anything astronomical, but they managed to build up enough of a following for a steady stream to trickle in from advertising and donations. After this quick success, Roberta and James were brought officially into the fold. The company had direction now and —while it remained secondary to each of their full-time careers—there was the shared hope it could turn into something more. Especially for Ken. In all his years, Tony had never known a man so driven to prove the existence of the impossible.

James finished his drink and smacked his lips together. 'God, the ale tastes so much better up here.' He wiped his mouth on his shirt sleeve. 'My round. Same again, everyone?' He didn't wait for an answer and squeezed past Roberta, exited the booth, and made his way over to the bar.

'I'm so sorry about him,' Roberta said with a small laugh as she tucked a strand of dark hair behind her ear. She was a very attractive girl, with classical Mediterranean features: long dark hair, olive skin, and blue eyes. A short girl at only five-foot-four, Tony knew better than to under estimate her based on her height. He had seen Roberta lose her temper on a few occasions and didn't envy anyone on the other side of her ire. 'I guess he's excited.'

'It's good to be enthusiastic,' Ken said, 'we just need to make sure we keep focused. I'm not kidding when I say this next week is going to be difficult. When we're all tired and grouchy and cold and hungry, the novelty will soon wear off.'

'We know that,' Roberta said with an ever-so-slightly defensive tone. 'We know what we signed up for. But I do think James has a point. We have a full week in a location like this... there's a chance we may get something.'

Tony wasn't sure he shared Roberta's optimism, given their lack of uncovering anything concrete over the past five years. Even the stranger things they had seen and experienced could either be easily dismissed by people of a mind to do so, or they hadn't been properly recorded—such as the disembodied voice begging for help Tony had heard at Hobbes Hall in Northern England. What little they uncovered had been enough to gather viewers to their social media account, but it wasn't enough to push them to the next level. There was nothing they had found that really separated the company from the scores of others who were doing the same thing.

And some of them even faked it to advance their audience. It was something Ken in particular abhorred.

'I do hope you're right,' Ken said and rubbed at his thick neck. In his early fifties, grey had stripped the vibrant black colour from his hair, which on his head was scraggly and pulled back into a ponytail. His thick moustache and beard gave him the appearance of an older Hells Angel, but his dress sense was more checkered shirts, multi-pocketed body warmers, shorts, and hiking boots. Definitely an outdoorsman, which was good, considering what they were about to embark upon.

Roberta shrugged. 'All we can do is try, then put out whatever we find. Even if it's nothing, I think what we are doing here will be well received: a documented week in a supposedly haunted forest—where people have gone missing, no less. That's gotta be a huge draw.'

'And then there's the legend of the lost village,' Tony added, finishing off his own drink.

'Exactly,' Roberta responded, eyes widening in excitement. 'The legend itself is interesting enough. I can't believe it's not more well known in the supernatural community.'

'Well,' Ken began, scratching at his beard, 'you'd be surprised how much folklore is out there that's been all but forgotten. The internet holds a lot of information, but it doesn't know everything.'

'Well, maybe not yet,' Roberta answered. 'But it's gonna know a lot more about the Black Forest when we're done.'

'Hey,' James shouted over to them from the bar, a row of drinks lined up before him. He was standing beside the ancient-looking gentleman perched on the stool. 'This guy knows about the Black Forest, and even the lost village.' James was pointing at the old man, whose expression was unreadable. 'For a few drinks, he says he'll tell us all he knows.'

Ken gave Tony a disapproving look and shook his head. 'That's okay,' Ken shouted back. 'I think we know all we need to.'

'Nonsense,' James responded. 'I've already bought him a drink, so we are good to go.' James then expertly gathered up the four drinks for his table and headed back to them, motioning for the stranger to follow. The man slowly slipped down from his stool and shuffled over, his back hunched as he did, a fresh, new pint of black liquid clutched in his claw-like hand. His clothes—plain trousers, a black shirt, and wool coat—looked too big for his light frame, and the sleeping dog didn't even stir as his master left. James set the drinks down and pulled up a chair for their guest.

'His name is Alistair,' James said as the man slowly sat down. 'Tell my friends what you told me.' He then turned back to the rest of the group. 'You gotta hear this. Talk about setting the tone. Go ahead, Alistair, tell them.'

The old man shook his head wearily and took a slow sip as the others waited for him to speak. When he did, his accent was a thick, harsh Scottish one. 'You're making a mistake going out there,' he said. 'And chances are, you won't be coming back.'

James let out a laugh. 'Can you believe that? It's straight out of a bad horror film. We've got to get that on camera. Roberta, get your phone out and record him.'

James seemed to be getting off on the stranger's ominous warning, but when Tony looked Alistair in the eyes, he didn't see a ranting drunk, or attention seeker, or anything of that nature, only a tiredness of someone who had seen things in life he had never wanted to.

Alistair held Tony's gaze and leaned in closer to him alone. 'Listen to me, lad,' Alistair said in a hushed whisper. 'The Black Woods ain't somewhere you want to be going. It ain't a place for the living.'

2

'Roberta,' Ken said, calmly but forcefully. 'Please put your phone away. We don't need any of this on video.'

'Why not?' James asked. 'This is good stuff, and the viewers would want to see it. It adds a bit of backstory.'

'We'll be fine without it,' Ken stated. 'We don't want to embarrass him online.'

'I'll just get perm—'

'James!' Ken snapped. 'Just leave it. Talk to him if you must, but we aren't going to record an inebriated old man and then splash him all over the internet to be made fun of.' Ken then turned to the man in question. 'No offence.'

The man just shrugged. 'No offence taken, lad.'

'Fine,' James huffed, slouching in his seat and crossing his arms. Roberta slid the phone she had retrieved back into her pocket.

Ken was getting annoyed with the whole charade and felt a pang of anger worm its way up from his gut. He'd told them all time and time again that the next week was going to be tough, but it seemed his words were falling on deaf ears. James, in particular, just didn't want to listen. Instead of the group focusing on the work ahead, the whole thing was being treated like a holiday, a bit of fun—rather than a serious project.

Tonight had supposed to have been a few quiet drinks, and then early to bed, ready for tomorrow—ready for work. Instead, James was getting drunk.

They were actually drinking in the same place they would be staying—the closest place to the Black Forest Ken could find given Amaley was the nearest town. Even then, it was a twenty-minute drive to the outskirts of the forest, so Ken wanted to be up early and checked out in good time.

He knew he needed to draw the distraction with the old man to a close, get their remaining drinks finished, and send everyone to bed.

'You should listen to me, you know,' Alistair said. 'Nothing good can come of you lot going out there.'

Tony cut in this time. 'So what do you know of the Black Forest, then? We've managed to uncover a lot of the local legend, I believe, but I'd be interested in finding out if there is anything we've missed.'

'Let me ask you,' Alistair replied, shuffling his seat closer to the table. 'Why do you want to go there, anyway? What is of interest to you? It's just a forest—an old, unforgiving place. There's nothing for tourists there. Come to think of it, there's nothing for tourists here in Amaley, either. Bit far off the beaten track, ain't ya?'

Tony nodded. 'I guess. But that's kind of the point. We investigate legends and folklore, things like that, and document what we find. Everything we find, we put up on the web for people to watch, so they can draw their own conclusions.'

'The web?'

'The internet,' James clarified. 'Surely you've heard of the internet?'

'Course I have,' Alistair replied, curling his top lip. 'I ain't stupid. Never had much use for it myself, though. And never heard it called the web before.'

'Well,' Tony interjected, 'that's what we do. And that's why we're here.'

'You looking for ghosts, lad?'

Tony shrugged. 'I guess that wouldn't be a bad thing to find.'

Alistair let out a humourless chuckle. 'Oh yes, it would. It would be very bad.'

'What makes you say that?' Roberta asked. 'Why would it be bad?'

Alistair took a long drink, which left foamy residue on his lips. The old man didn't wipe it away, however, content instead to let it stay put, like a white, frothy moustache. 'People go in there and don't come back. Happened a lot through the years. Less now, of course, cos people have the good sense to stay away. Don't get much in the way of hikers out here nowadays. Haven't in a while. That's a good thing. Do yourselves a favour and go investigate someplace else.'

'But people going missing isn't unusual,' James cut in. 'It happens all the time, even in small towns. And people getting lost in the woods and not turning up happens more often than you'd think as well. The last instance we could find of people going missing out in those woods was a group of hikers back in 2001.'

'Well, you've got your facts wrong, ain't ya, boy.' There was a touch of annoyance in the old man's voice. Ken squinted his eyes as he listened intently. If there had been others that had gone missing since the turn of the century, then Ken hadn't heard anything. Alistair went on. 'People from this town have disappeared. Called into that forest by the Devil himself. Or rather, his disciple—that evil bitch Mother Sibbett. And when the call comes, that's it for you. You don't come back. People around these parts know it, but never talk about it. Like to ignore it and pretend it isn't real. But it's real, all right.'

Ken felt the eyes of the others land on him. 'You know anything about any others going missing, boss?' James asked.

Ken shook his head.

'Well it's true,' Alistair stated. 'Sure as I'm sitting here with you.'

'And what about the village?' Roberta asked. 'Do you know any of the stories about the village that people say once stood in those woods?'

Alistair studied her face with his pale blue eyes before slowly nodding. 'That was an old, old village. Existed a long time ago. Swallowed up by the woods now.'

'Well,' James said, 'apparently no one has been able to find any trace of it. So most just think it's an urban legend.'

'Most are wrong,' Alistair replied. 'That village was settled in the sixteen-hundreds, in a clearing in the forest—so the story goes. Lasted for less than fifty years. People who lived there went mad, their minds poisoned by Mother Sibbett and the evil she obeyed. Something dark and ancient lives in those woods and it turned once-good people into something... different. Made them commit acts against God. And their souls are still up there, I think, waiting to carry out the twisted bidding of Sibbett and those evil things she worshipped.'

James downed the rest of his drink. 'Sorry, Ken,' he said, 'but we should be getting this on film. We still have signal here and could upload something online tonight. It's a perfect hook, in case we don't have the opportunity to put out anything until the investigation is over. This alone will get people interested. I mean, hell, it's like the start of a bad horror story. People will love it.' James turned to Alistair. 'Can you repeat all that—on camera, if that's okay?'

Ken was quickly losing patience with being ignored. 'James! For the last time, I said no. I'm not going to cheapen this whole thing and turn it into some fake shit that is only aimed at getting ratings. We will report what we know, factually, and see what we find. We need this to be taken seriously.'

Ken saw James look to Roberta, and then to Tony, for backup. To Ken's surprise, Tony looked like he was about to say something, but in the end remained quiet.

'Fine,' James replied, still sounding petulant.

Ken turned to the old man, who was busy gulping down a hearty mouthful of his drink. 'I think we already know most of what we need to. My family originated from around here, so my grandparents were aware of the stories and legends. And I do thank you for your help and words of warning, but I'm sure we'll be fine out there. We know what we are getting ourselves into, and we are prepared.'

The suddenness and forcefulness of Alistair's resulting laugh shocked them all. 'You ain't prepared for what's waiting! You ain't prepared at all! Bunch of blind know-it-alls getting in over their heads. Not gonna end well for you, I can tell ya that for sure.'

'Either way,' Ken said, firmly, 'we thank you for your time. Now please excuse us.'

The old man finished his drink and shook his head. 'Suit yourselves. I guess I'll be reading about you in the newspapers after you go missing.' With that, he got to his feet and slowly shuffled away from their table, passing the barman on his way and heading to a rather narrow door that led to the toilets.

'Going to drain the vein!' Alistair shouted over to the barman. 'Line me up another while I'm gone, will you?'

The barman nodded, but before he did as instructed, made his way over to the group. A short-sleeved white shirt stretched over the man's impressive gut, and buttons that seemed to be losing their fight to fasten it together threatened to ping off in all directions. Both of the man's meaty forearms were covered in tattoos, and he sported a rather wild handlebar moustache. When he reached the table, he began to gather up their empty glasses.

'Can I get any of you another?' the barman asked with an accent just as thick as Alistair's had been. James looked like he was about to answer, but Ken did so for all of them.

'No, thank you, I think we will be calling it a night. Early start tomorrow.'

'No problem,' the barman replied. 'Couldn't help but overhear you folks talking to old Alistair. Hope he didn't frighten you too much.'

'I can assure you he didn't,' Ken told the barman.

'Good. He likes to spin a yarn, Alistair does. Tells everyone that will listen—and even those that won't. Not saying that there aren't some strange goings-on up in the Black Forest, but I'm not inclined to believe it's as bad as he makes out.'

'What sort of goings-on?' Roberta asked.

'Well, what he said about there being no hikers up here in years? That was a lie. We had a group up here last year, no less. They stayed with us, and after their hike in the woods they all came back just fine. Not as chatty as when they'd left, mind you, but all of them travelled back home safely, and in one piece to boot.'

'So why would Alistair say all that?' James asked.

'He loves an audience and likes to scare people. Just the way he is.'

'So everything he said was a lie?' Tony asked.

'Oh, God no. Most of it was true. Just embellished a little. He's also right about one thing in particular—the place is unforgiving. The weather can turn nasty up here with no notice. Anyone that's gone missing or died in the woods was likely stricken by things much more natural than ghosts or demons. It's a big forest, and there's no way to contact the outside world. Not much in the way of rescue all the way up here. So, you should be very careful, I'll say that much.'

With all of the glasses gathered up, he trundled back over to the bar.

'Okay,' Ken said. 'I think we've had enough excitement today. So, if no one has any complaints, I say we call it a night and turn in. We have a long day tomorrow and need to get an early start. I'd like to be checked out of here and en route to the Black Forest before nine a.m. That okay with everyone?' Ken looked at James specifically as he spoke. James glared back, but eventually nodded.

'Sure.'

Ken looked around to everyone else and received the same compliant nods. 'Excellent. Then let's go.'

The group stood up as one and made their way to the door that led to the staircase. Their warm rooms and beds awaited, and it would likely be the last comfortable night's sleep they would have for a week, so Ken hoped they all savoured it.

'Good night,' the barman called as they passed him. Ken, last in line, gave the man a friendly wave and smile.

He didn't want to get ahead of himself, and he knew that

the likelihood was they would find little-to-nothing in the way of credible evidence, but still, he hoped and prayed that their investigation would turn something up. He'd been doing this a long time and was no closer to proving the existence of life after death.

And he dearly wanted to change that. He *needed* to.

3

'OKAY,' Tony said, looking through the camera's viewfinder. 'That's good.'

He stepped around the tripod and joined his three colleagues, standing just in front of the tree line to the Black Forest. As per Ken's instructions the previous night, the group had risen early—too early for James, it seemed, who was nursing a headache—and devoured a hearty breakfast that consisted of crispy bacon, baked beans, poached eggs, mixed toast, hash browns, and black pudding. The portions were generous, and Ken was the only one who managed to clean his plate. After washing it all down with steaming mugs of hot, rich coffee, the group felt refreshed and ready for the day ahead. The breakfast had even perked up James, to some extent.

From there, they had all bundled into Ken's Mitsubishi SUV and made the twenty-minute drive out of Amaley to the edges of the Black Forest. The last four miles had been little more than a dirt track. Upon arriving, James had questioned whether Ken was comfortable leaving his car out there in the open for a whole week—on the cusp between forest and fields. Ken had replied in the affirmative, and then guided the vehicle behind a section of high grass and bushes. It wasn't completely hidden, but it was something.

And now they were about to film the opening sequence to their investigation. Tony had set up a small video camera on a sturdy tripod, framed the shot, and now stood with the rest of them.

Ken then launched into the opening dialogue they had all practiced on the drive over. 'Greetings from the edges of the Black Forest, all the way up here in Northern Scotland. The team is well rested and ready for what lies ahead.'

'That's right,' Roberta picked up. 'We've come up here to investigate one of the strangest and scariest pieces of folk-lore in British history. But, surprisingly, it may not be one you are familiar with.'

'It isn't widely known,' James went on, 'but these woods have a long record of strange events. And, for those in the know, it is supposedly one of the most haunted spots in the United Kingdom. Stories of ghost sightings, disembodied voices, and supernatural activity abound. But worse, over twenty people have vanished after entering these woods in the last seventy years alone. And those are just the ones we know about.'

Tony stepped in next. 'And it all starts, supposedly, with the story of a village. Established within these woods in the sixteen-hundreds, the unnamed village is said to have vanished after its inhabitants were driven mad. Rumours of extreme occult activity—ritual sacrifice, deviant sexual acts, and the worshipping of dark deities—spread to the local towns, including the one we stayed in last night, Amaley. The surrounding population turned their back on the small village, cutting it off, and renounced the vile gospel the town tried to spread. After six years with no contact, groups from Amaley and another town entered the Black Forest, hoping to find out what had happened to their neighbours. They split into two groups, and the first searched as much of the woods as possible, even managing to find the remains of the town. But things there were not as they should be. On top of that, the second group vanished, never to be seen again.'

Ken took a deliberate step forward. 'The history of this forest is a long one, and we will have much more information on our website and in the show notes. But given the extensive reports of activity throughout the years, we are hopeful that our week-long stay in this forest will provide us with the one thing we are searching for: irrefutable proof of the supernatural—to know for certain that there is more to this life than we are currently aware of. Welcome to our investigation.' Ken then turned to Tony and gave a subtle nod. *We're done.*

But Tony knew that Ken wasn't quite finished, as much as he'd like to have been. Tony gave a faint shake of his head, and Ken rolled his eyes before looking back to the camera. 'This,' he said, dramatically, 'is Paranormal Encounters.'

They all held their pose for a second before James broke ranks with a quick clap. 'That's great,' he said with a big smile. 'I think it flowed really naturally. And you are getting bloody good at delivering that catchphrase, Ken.'

'I hate the catchphrase,' Ken replied.

James shrugged. 'They help. All the main players in the game have one. At least it's not as bad as the one The Ghoul Hunters use. The *para*normal *is* our *normal*. Please. It sounds terrible.'

Ken just shook his head with a scowl, and Tony had to hold back a chuckle. He knew with certainty that, in Ken's head, they both sounded as bad as each other. And he had a point.

Then again, so did James.

'Let's get the camera packed up and start moving,' Ken said.

They did as instructed, and—once all were ready— stood before the forest again, this time looking into the mass of trees before them. They could hear sounds of wildlife, and the canopy of branches and leaves above blotted out much of the light, lending an ominous feeling to the surrounding area. Tony felt a small shiver creep its way up his spine. He couldn't decide if it was nerves or excitement, but he was anxious to get going regardless.

'Are we ready?' James asked.

'Yes,' Ken replied. 'Let's go.'

With that, they set off. The Black Forest swallowed them up as they crossed its threshold.

4

THE BACKPACK WAS heavy and uncomfortable on James' back. It contained the tent that he and Roberta would share, as well as their clothes. Roberta was carrying their food, their sleeping bags, and some of the filming equipment. Though she was carrying about the same amount of weight as James, she didn't seem to be showing the same signs of fatigue, marching on ahead like a machine. James couldn't help but watch her arse as it swayed before him, pushed out against the grey cargo trousers she was wearing and almost hypnotic in its movement. That sight alone helped take his mind off his aching back and the soreness of his feet as his new hiking boots nipped at the skin.

Why the hell didn't I break these in beforehand?

The air around him seemed different than that of his hometown—fresher and sharper. It was probably just in his head, but the smell of the mossy earth, fallen leaves, and pine from the trees made the whole area smell... cleaner... than the urban environment he was used to. It was refreshing, but the air also burned his lungs as they hiked onwards, treading over twigs and fallen branches that snapped underfoot.

James, while tired, had a hugely positive feeling about the upcoming week. This trip would set them apart from the competition—they weren't simply settling for one night in a haunted location; this was a full week of throwing themselves into their job and recording everything. Even if they picked up very little in terms of actual evidence, he knew with careful editing they could put together something really intriguing that their audience would devour. They just needed to give it some kind of structure and narrative, which would be fuelled by the legend and history attached to the forest itself. That was the key to it all, James knew, and the fact that Ken had stopped him filming the old man from the pub last night still annoyed him.

All they needed was Alistair's verbal approval on film, and they could have used the footage and the story he told. It was great stuff, more than they could have hoped for: the story of the Black Forest as told by a local, and with an ominous tone as well.

Instead, it was a wasted opportunity. And James had seen a lot of those during his short time at Paranormal Encounters.

If they were to survive—well, not just survive, but thrive —then Ken needed to embrace a few of the more 'modern' methods of hooking audiences. And given Ken's stubbornness, James knew that would be difficult; he would need backup to pressure Ken into seeing things his way. Getting Roberta on board wouldn't be too difficult, he hoped, but the tricky one would be Tony.

Tony, to James, was a walking stereotype of normality. Average height, in decent shape for a forty-something, black hair still styled in a side part despite it not being the fifties.

His face was also unremarkable: not strikingly handsome and certainly not ugly, but decidedly middle-of-the-road. Tony was eminently sensible, reasoned, and level-headed.

But he was also loyal, especially to Ken.

Regardless, as far as James could see it was their esteemed leader who, while knowledgeable in matters of the paranormal, was still the weak link of the group.

James, for example, knew marketing. He knew how to put their brand together and get it out there. Roberta was very technically gifted, and—given her degree in film and media—adept at using filming equipment. It was a new world, and since both James and Roberta were in their early thirties, they were best placed to understand it. Tony, for his part, was quite well versed in the paranormal and other phenomena. Perhaps not as much as Ken, but he certainly seemed to know his onions. He was also the 'glue' of the group, or peacemaker, and helped the team function whenever there were disagreements. He could fill in and set his hands to most tasks, performing at least adequately.

James let himself smirk, feeling sorry for Tony's wife if *adequate* was the best she could hope for. He couldn't imagine the poor girl had ever felt any sort of toe-curling passion with *Mr. Meh*.

But Mr. Meh could be useful, and an asset to the company.

Ken, on the other hand, simply served to hold them all back, director of the company or not. He was always the one averse to trying new things, pushing the envelope, or actually trying to turn this endeavour into a legitimate business. All he cared about was doing things by the book.

But this was ghost-hunting, for Christ's sake. The book was hardly set in stone.

James was so deep in thought that he didn't see Roberta

stop walking in front of him, causing him to bump into the back of her.

'Watch where you're going,' she scolded.

'Sorry. Why have we stopped?'

Roberta pointed up ahead. Ken was stationary, as was the rest of their line, looking out amongst the trees beyond to the top of an incline.

'Yo, Ken!' James shouted. He never got the chance to add to that, as he was quickly shushed by the older man, who had his head cocked to one side.

Ken was listening.

The rest of the group remained silent. James tried to focus in on whatever it was Ken was hearing, or had heard, but he couldn't detect a thing—only the natural sounds of the forest wildlife. Chirping, buzzing, and the calls of unknown animals, all in the distance. And all, as far as James was concerned, completely normal.

'I could have sworn...' Ken started, but trailed off, again listening intently. Eventually, however, he shook his head with a scowl.

'What is it?' Tony asked.

'I'm almost certain I heard it. Off in the distance.'

'Heard what?' It was Roberta's turn to ask.

Ken looked at each of them, then off again into the trees. 'A person,' he said at last. 'The sound was faint, far away, but I'm sure of what I heard. At least, I think I am. It was a kind of moan. The sound of someone in pain.'

'Are you sure it wasn't just the wind?' James asked, though he was aware there was only a gentle breeze blowing around them. It wasn't enough to make much of a sound, or whistle through the branches.

Ken's shoulders fell a little. 'I don't think so, but who knows.'

James, doubtful Ken had actually heard anything, but thinking quickly anyway, grabbed his small handheld camera. Each of them carried one in case they needed to get something while on the move. James snapped the viewfinder open and walked over to Ken. 'Okay,' he said, aiming the camera at the company director, 'we're only a few hours into our expedition, and already we have something. Ken Chambers, the founder of Paranormal Encounters, just heard a strange voice off in the distance. Ken, can you tell the viewers exactly what the sound was?'

Ken looked right past the camera to James and sighed. 'Not now,' he said. 'Get that out of my face. We'll get some footage a little later.'

James stopped recording and lowered the camera, but did not close the viewfinder. He shook his head and let his own annoyance show.

'For God's sake, Ken, this is why we're here. I know you're averse to this kind of thing, but guess what? That's the name of the game. We investigate and film what we find. This is *exactly* what we need to be getting. It's what we signed up for, so will you please get over yourself and talk to the camera?'

Ken looked furious, but James didn't care. What he'd said was nothing but the truth. If Ken was so against talking about these things, why was he even here?

'We don't have anything,' Ken answered. 'Like you said, it could have been the wind, for all we know. It's nothing we can prove, just a noise I heard.'

'You seemed pretty sure it was a voice.'

'I thought it was.'

'Then tell us about it.' James threw his hands up in the air, and then looked to Tony for backup. To his surprise, he actually got it.

'He's right, Ken,' Tony said. Ken looked as surprised as James felt. 'You don't have to say it is anything concrete, but just describe what you heard. That's all. Put it out there for what it is. Nothing more.'

Ken remained silent for a moment. 'Did you hear anything?' he asked Tony.

Tony shook his head. 'No, but that doesn't mean it wasn't there. To be honest, I wasn't really paying attention.'

Ken stared down at his boots and chewed his lip. 'Fine,' he eventually said, then looked up. 'Whenever you are ready.'

'Great,' James replied with a smile. He aimed the camera back at Ken and quickly ran through another introduction, before asking, 'So, Ken, can you tell the viewers exactly what you heard?'

Ken took a moment, looked into the camera, then began. 'As we were walking, I heard a faint sound up ahead. Though I can't be one-hundred-percent certain, it did seem to me like a pained moan. It definitely didn't sound like the normal noises of the forest. And while it's nothing concrete and could be explainable, it is something. Enough to keep us on our toes, at least, and a reminder to keep our ears and eyes open.'

James nodded and spun the camera around to face himself. 'Wow, what a start! Like Ken says, possibly explainable, but we'll hope to get much more in the hours and days ahead. This is just the beginning. And not only that—'

James suddenly stopped and whipped his head up, scarcely able to believe the sound he was now picking up.

It appeared that Ken had been right.

5

AFTER HEARING THOSE PAINED, distant cries, Roberta found herself rooted to the spot for a moment... but only for a moment. She soon realised that whatever was happening needed to be recorded, in film if possible.

James had his camera pointing off into the distance, towards the direction of the unnerving sounds, but the audio quality on a simple handheld camera with no external microphone would be lousy at best.

The haunting noises went on, seemingly drifting towards them on the light breeze, and Roberta slipped off her rucksack, dug inside, and retrieved a short, boom-style mic. She then quickly moved over to Tony, who was nearest, and grabbed his handheld camera before plugging the mic into it.

'Hold this up with the camera,' she said. 'Record what you can.' Mouth agape at what they were hearing, Tony gave a nod and did as instructed. Roberta then went back to her equipment and quickly found her handheld digital audio recorder.

'This is unbelievable,' James said, his voice little more

than a whisper. Roberta quickly slung on her backpack and stepped beside him, then lifted up her recording device. 'What do we do?' James asked.

'Find out where it's coming from,' Ken said.

Roberta was already on the same page, as pursuit was the obvious choice. Which is why she hadn't taken the time to set up any of the bigger, high-quality equipment that could pick up the sounds with more clarity; they needed to be quick and agile here.

Though, in listening to the faint yet undeniable cries of pain, Roberta would be lying to herself if she said she wasn't a little hesitant. The voice seemed to be coming from a single person—a male—and if it was actually someone in danger who needed help, there was a chance that danger could find them too.

If it was something else entirely—the very thing they were here looking for—then that brought its own fears, too. Roberta had looked into many cases with Paranormal Encounters and was certainly a believer. Even though they had never found anything mind-blowing, she was always nervous during investigations and had no idea how she would react if she actually *did* see something. That was always the difficulty for her. She wanted desperately to find something, but in the moment things were happening, she was generally relieved when they came up empty-handed. It wasn't until after, when the fear had subsided, that the inevitable disappointment reared its head.

And now, listening to this... could it actually be something? Was Roberta about to see the thing that she both craved and feared?

'Follow me,' Ken whispered, then began walking forward, taking slow and steady steps. The rest of them followed, losing the shape of the single-file line they had been keeping as they bunched together, allowing the cameras and digital audio recorder to pick up what whatever they could, unobstructed.

Leaves, foliage, and twigs crunched underfoot. The forest was not a dense one, and the trunks of the trees were relatively thin, but it stretched out seemingly forever in each direction. They had been walking through the forest for a few hours already, and Roberta was aware that, with each step, the group was becoming more and more isolated.

Just what were they walking into?

They kept on going. Five minutes, ten, then twenty— always following the sound. One that didn't seem to be getting any louder. Roberta suddenly spun after hearing something directly behind her. A whisper, saying her own name, and it was so close she could have sworn she'd felt a cold breath displace her hair. But there was nothing.

She sighed and shook her head, thankful she had refrained from shouting out in fright, which could have embarrassed her in front of the others.

Don't let yourself get creeped out.

Roberta knew that she was just letting her mind run away with itself and that she had to focus, and not let herself get spooked. This was just another investigation, nothing more. It was then she felt something cold and wet drop on her head. She quickly looked up, and saw on a tree above a string of thick liquid falling from a branch. The gasp that came out of her was ill-timed, and Roberta felt the thick substance splashing against her tongue. She quickly sidestepped, gagging and coughing, as more dripped to the forest floor, but inadvertently swallowed some of the foul-tasting fluid in the process.

'What's the matter?' she heard James ask.

Robert continued to cough and spit as she pointed up

above. Everyone gathered round and Roberta, when she had managed to get her gagging under control, saw that the branches of the tree that the liquid was falling from looked black-almost like they had been burned. 'I swallowed some,' she said, feeling disgusted. The taste in her mouth was awful and—whether it was her mind playing tricks, she wasn't sure—Roberta could almost feel a glob of the stuff fall into her stomach.

Tony bent down and examined the liquid, grabbing at some of it between his fingers. As he spread the digits apart, the substance held together and stretched out in strings.

'Possibly sap,' he said.

'What sort of sap is black?' James asked, but Tony just shrugged, not knowing the answer.

'Are you okay?' Ken asked Roberta.

'I think so,' she replied. 'But I definitely swallowed some. Will it make me sick?'

'How much went down?'

'Only a little.'

Ken paused to think for a moment. 'Drink plenty of water,' he said. 'I don't think it can do you much harm, but let us know if you start to feel ill.'

Roberta nodded and took long pulls from her water flask, spitting some of it back out in an attempt to rid her mouth of that horrible, sour taste. Eventually, she gave them a thumbs up and they started walking again.

'Are we even going the right way?' James asked not long after they set off.

'I thought so,' Ken answered. 'But we don't seem to be getting any closer.'

'We should be, though,' Tony added. 'We are definitely heading towards the noise, I'm certain of that. But the cries still sound faint, as if they are still a ways away.'

James nodded his agreement. 'And that's not normal, right?'

'No,' Ken said. 'I don't believe it is.'

They walked for just shy of another ten minutes before Ken held up his hand and drew them to a stop.

'Notice anything?' Ken asked. Roberta did and was about to raise the point right before Ken stopped them.

'It's gone,' Tony said. 'The sound is gone.'

Roberta wasn't sure when exactly that had happened.

For the last few minutes, the subtle cries of pain had seemed to get quieter and quieter, but now they had phased out altogether, becoming lost in the natural sounds of the forest.

They continued to listen for a little while before Roberta switched off her recorder. Tony followed suit, flipping shut the viewfinder on his camera and unplugging the mic. James, however, turned his camera around, to once again face himself.

'Well, I guess we can all confirm what Ken heard earlier. The sound of someone, seemingly in pain, was clear to all of us. We followed it as best we could, but never seemed to get any closer. As you may have heard, the noise has apparently stopped, but it was certainly unsettling to hear. Hopefully our equipment picked it all up. Right now, we're all wondering the same thing: was this our first supernatural encounter here in the Black Forest?'

He raised his eyebrows as he finished, letting the question hang before switching his camera off. A big grin spread across his face. 'That was fucking awesome.'

Roberta wasn't sure she agreed with him, and she could still feel the hairs on the back of her neck standing on end. Whoever was the source of those cries was undoubtedly in pain—whether alive or dead, they were suffering, and she couldn't help feel the group should take it as a warning.

'It was certainly interesting,' Tony admitted.

Roberta shivered. 'And really fucking creepy.'

'Yeah, I agree,' Tony replied, surprising her. 'Definitely freaked me out a little. But it had to be something paranormal. Right, Ken?'

Ken was still surveying the area around them, scratching at his greying, scruffy beard with a large hand. 'Well, we can't say for certain,' he answered. 'But we definitely can't rule it out.' Roberta actually saw a hint of a smile creep over his face, which was a rarity. 'It might just be, though. We can review the audio when we stop for lunch.'

'Speaking of which,' Roberta said, feeling her stomach growl. The internal organ seemed to have a mind of its own and reacted almost immediately at the mention of lunch. 'When will that be? I feel like I could eat a whole cow.'

'Well, be careful to stick to your ration portions,' Ken said. 'Otherwise, you'll be eating leaves the second half of the week. But I guess we could stop now.' He looked around and pointed a little way ahead. 'There seems to be a small clearing over there. Looks as good a place as any.'

They walked the few hundred yards to the spot Ken had found and began taking off their packs. The feeling of the weight falling from Roberta's back was heavenly, as if her shoulders were rising up of their own accord. James let out an audible groan of pleasure.

'I'm going to be sore as hell, lugging that thing around all week,' he said as he rubbed the side of his neck before letting himself drop to the ground next to his discarded pack. He stretched out and groaned again.

Roberta giggled. 'Don't over-exaggerate. They aren't *that* heavy.'

James rolled over and propped himself up onto one elbow. He gave a smile. 'Mine is, but I'm probably carrying more than you, given my hulking, manly body.' He flexed a rather thin arm, theatrically. 'So I think you should come ease my aching muscles.'

'I don't think any of us want to see that,' Tony cut in, chuckling.

James shrugged. 'Suppose you're right.'

Ken squatted down and began to dig through his own pack. 'For now, I recommend we just eat something quick. We can set up the stove tonight and have something a little more hearty when we stop to camp.'

As much as Roberta felt like she could eat their whole supply of rations at that moment, they all agreed, and instead Roberta indulged in a tin of tuna she ate with her fingers, a chocolate bar, and a packet of mixed nuts—all washed down with a little water from her flask. It was a meagre feed and did little to quell the insatiable hunger that seemed to gnaw at her, but it at least replenished a little more strength.

They all finished at roughly the same time and remained seated in the circle they had formed. Ken and Tony sat on fallen logs, Roberta nestled at the base of a tree, and James rested on the ground beside her.

'So,' Ken said. 'What say we check out a little of what we recorded earlier?'

'I'm all eyes and ears,' James said, sitting a bit more upright.

Ken looked to Roberta. 'Would you do the honours, please?'

Roberta nodded. 'Sure thing. I'll check the digital recorder, see if we got any of the sounds on there.'

She unfurled her earbuds from her pocket and plugged

them into the device. Starting from the beginning of the recorded audio, she listened intently. James plugged his own earphones into his camera and also checked the footage.

Roberta heard the distorted, pounding noise of the wind —which had in fact been very light—hit against the device's microphone, making it sound much worse than it had actually been. This was one of the inevitable pitfalls of recording sound outdoors, but Roberta knew she could clear most of that up in post-production with her editing equipment.

She listened for something more, however, hoping to pick something up in amongst the distortion.

Then she heard it. Her eyes went wide. Roberta looked over to see that James had a similar expression on his face. He ripped the earphones out of his ears.

'We've got it!' he shouted. 'You can hear that creepy fucking wailing on here. It's unmistakable. I can't believe it. We actually have some evidence, and we're only a few hours in.'

Ken held up a hand. 'Now, now,' he said. 'We don't know exactly what it is yet.' Despite his words of caution, Roberta could see that their leader was not able to conceal his own smile.

6

EVEN THOUGH IT stung his cheek, the fire felt good against Tony's skin. Given they were only just approaching autumn, the weather so far had not been nearly as bad as they'd feared. But even so, now that night was setting in, there was a noticeable chill to the air.

The remainder of the day, after the initial excitement, had been uneventful. There was plenty of walking, taking in the sights that the Black Forest had to offer, and Tony had on more than one occasion felt a sense of peace and contentment he'd not known before, simply by getting closer to nature. It wasn't a lifestyle he could keep up permanently, of course, as he was far too used to his creature comforts, but as a novelty it certainly gave him a new appreciation for the world around him.

At around six in the evening, Ken had made the call to stop and set up camp for the evening. They had found a relatively large clearing with plenty of room for their tents, and the canopy from the trees above gave them plenty of shelter, which would help if rain set in.

They had assembled the tents quite efficiently given

they were all—except Ken—relative amateurs to camping, with James having the most trouble with his two-person tent. He stoutly refused any help, even from Roberta, who would be sharing it with him. Once that task was completed and their sleeping bags and equipment were all stored inside, they set to work building a fire by gathering up as many dry branches, twigs, and leaves as they could, then dumping them into the centre of a circle of stones that they had formed. Thankfully, the group didn't need to resort to rubbing dry sticks together to spark a flame, as both Tony and Ken had brought cheap, disposable lighters, so it didn't take long for the fire to take hold and leap up to an impressive height.

As they all warmed themselves by it, sitting in a circle, Ken busied himself setting up the camping stove. The meal that night would consist of only rice and beans, but at least it would be warm, and there would be more than a few mouthfuls. To Tony, that sounded like a feast. Dusk had taken hold, and the natural daylight was failing.

'So, Ken,' James began, 'do you have a good feeling about what we've experienced already?'

The stove was erected, and Ken was pouring beans into the metal cooking pot. 'We'll see,' he replied. 'I won't deny the events from earlier excited me... somewhat. Certainly not the start I was expecting. But let's see what the rest of the week brings.'

'Fair enough,' James replied. 'Doesn't hurt to remain cautious, I suppose. But I think we will see even more tonight. This place is unreal. I think it's a hive of activity.'

'Hive of activity?' Roberta asked with a raised eyebrow and mocking smile. 'That a technical term?'

'As technical as any we use, I suppose. But you know

what I mean. To have something like that happen straight off the bat—I just know it's the tip of the iceberg for us.'

Tony tried to take Ken's approach and keep his expectations in check, but James' enthusiasm was infectious, and Tony couldn't help but hope for the same. What they'd recorded earlier was undoubtedly some of the most compelling evidence they had ever produced.

Ken stirred the beans as they started to cook and the smell wafted over to Tony, causing his mouth to salivate.

'Are we still on track, Ken?' Roberta asked, rubbing her hands together and holding them out towards the fire.

'In what regard?'

'I mean, do you know roughly where we are? We don't have a map, so we're trusting you to get us all out of here.'

'Yeah, I couldn't find much info on this area, despite my best efforts,' Ken acknowledged. 'But I'm keeping track of our direction—we are heading due east—and taking notes on how long we've walked, as well as jotting down any noticeable landmarks.'

Tony had already seen Ken stopping every so often, scribbling away in a small, pocket-sized notebook. This, he knew, was Ken's way of tracking their progress.

'Landmarks?' James asked. 'I see only trees. How can you tell them apart?'

'Well, there is more to it than that. There are fallen trees, different-sized logs, creeks, large rocks, and more. If you know what to look for then there are more than enough noticeable features we can use to track progress. And by keeping notes on how long we are walking in any given direction, coupled with these landmarks, we shouldn't have much trouble backtracking and getting out the same way we came in.'

Tony had no idea if it was a sound plan or not, but he

was putting his trust in Ken on the trip. They all were. And his answer seemed good enough to satisfy the others.

'Well, keep walking and we'll keep following, boss,' James said with an exaggerated salute.

'And what's the plan for tonight?' Tony asked. 'A vigil, or should we set up some equipment to run while we're all asleep?'

'I'll happily put that to a vote. What are everyone's thoughts?'

'We could set up some night-vision cameras,' Roberta said. 'We only have limited battery power, though, so it would be smart to set up only one. Maybe higher up in a tree to get a good view of the campsite.'

'We could stand vigil until the early hours,' James said, his enthusiasm still evident. 'Maybe call it a night at about three in the morning? That's always a good time for activity. Then run the cameras until we wake up.'

'Not a bad idea,' Ken said. 'But how is everyone feeling? We've hiked a lot today, and I'd wager it's something we're not all used to. Our bodies and minds are tired.'

Tony definitely agreed with him. Though the hiking hadn't exactly been strenuous, it had never-the-less been constant, and now that they had stopped to rest, Tony felt aches and pains spreading throughout his body.

'How about we stay awake as long as we feel up to it?' Tony suggested. 'Call it a night when our bodies tell us to. After all, we have to do it all again tomorrow. This is going to be a long week.'

'Agreed,' Roberta chimed in. 'We need to be sensible. Conserve our strength where we can. And sleep is going to be important for that.'

'Very sensible,' Ken said.

'Very boring,' James scoffed. 'But I see your point.'

'Sounds like we have our plan,' Ken confirmed.

They dished up the food for the evening and Tony took a taste from a generous portion that he'd lifted up on his fork. The food was basic, but tasted surprisingly good. His body ached for the nourishment and he greedily devoured everything from his tin container, even going so far as to lick the insides to make sure he had grabbed every last remaining grain of rice. As he set his container down and sucked in a mouthful of water, Tony saw that the others had inhaled their food just as quickly as he had.

A silence descended over the group as they sat and enjoyed the feeling of quelled hunger. Roberta snuggled against James, and all eyes stared into the flickering fire. Darkness was creeping in, snuffing out the last of the sunlight that broke through from the branches above. It would be a good idea to use this last light to set up any equipment they planned to use that night, but they all— Tony included—seemed content to simply sit and enjoy the brief period of rest and relaxation. Tony sat cross-legged on the ground but felt pins-and-needles prickle in his thigh and calf muscles, so he straightened out and instead lay on his side, relying on his waterproof jacket and trousers to keep any ground dampness at bay.

'Tell us about the history of the Black Forest again,' Roberta said to Ken. 'I remember what you've already told us, but I want to know more about how you came to find out about it. I still can't believe you grew up around this area. You don't have a Scottish accent at all.'

Ken chuckled. 'I moved down to England before I turned ten. My father followed the work, and in turn, the family followed him.'

'And you haven't been back here since?'

Ken shook his head. 'That's right. To be honest, I never

felt the need. I did most of my growing up away from here, so it's pretty much a distant memory.'

'So was Amaley your hometown?' James asked.

'No. I was from a place a little way from here, but we'd heard of Amaley, and the Black Forest. The local legend stretched out that far, at least. Of course, no one really believed much of it, but we knew that the forest was here. And I do remember the furor that swept the area when a couple went missing in those woods. I'd have been about six at the time, and it was all anyone seemed to talk about. That, and the old legend. Which makes sense, I suppose. That was the first time I heard it, from some friends at school, and after they told me I did some of my own research on the area and the stories that surrounded it. Some of it I got by way of books, but it was my uncle who told me the most, as he seemed pretty well versed. But after I moved away, I didn't think about Amaley or the Black Forest much more, and I never had the chance to speak to my uncle again. It was only when we were looking for somewhere big to investigate that the Black Forest popped back into my head.'

'So how come you couldn't find much about it online?' James asked. Tony already knew the answer, but listened intently anyway.

'Can't say for sure,' Ken responded. 'I managed to find little bits about the various disappearances, but that's all I could really uncover. There was the odd mention of a local legend, but no detail. However, I don't think it's that unusual, to be honest. There are thousands upon thousands of legends and pieces of folklore throughout the country, and not many get much in the way of publicity—and why should they?'

'Well, a lot of people have gone missing over the years,' Roberta said.

'But that's true of a lot of places,' Ken said. 'So, for what-ever reason, the story of the Black Forest never really trav-elled much past its place of origin.'

'I'm thankful for that,' James said. 'We can be the ones to uncover it. And, in the process, we can hit our audience with something new. The whole thing is perfect.'

'And your uncle was the one who told you the story?' Roberta asked Ken. 'About Mother Sibbett, the lost village, and even how the forest got its name?'

'Pretty much. Though it was backed up by what I heard from others when I lived here as well, especially in the after-math of the disappearances.'

'What was the first part of the story?' James asked. 'Go back as far as you can.' Before letting Ken answer, James clicked his fingers and shouted, 'Wait!' He was then up and moved over to his tent, ducking inside, only to come out with his camera. 'I know you aren't big on this kind of stuff, Ken, but this is a perfect way to get the story out to the audi-ence. When we upload all of this, they are going to want to know the backstory. And this is a good way to deliver it.' Ken made as if to speak, but James held up a finger. 'Before you say no, just think about it. We could write it all out and add a document to the show notes, sure, but video is our medium. And scary is our wheelhouse. What better way to get over the story of the Black Forest than by an honest-to-God campfire?'

'If you would have let me finish,' Ken said, smirking, 'I was about to say I agree with you.'

James raised his eyebrows. 'Holy shit, really?'

'Really.'

'That's awesome.' James flipped open the viewfinder. 'Now, we will need to get as close to you and the fire as possible for light, and also have to make sure the sound is okay. But the picture doesn't need to be perfect. If it's a little dark, that just adds to the ambience.'

Ken assumed his position while Tony and Roberta stood behind James, peering through his viewfinder. While the picture was dark, James was right—the flickering fire did create a creepy campfire effect. Tony had to give it to James, he had an eye for this kind of thing.

'Ready?' Ken asked.

James nodded. 'In your own time.'

Ken coughed, then began. 'We are told the town that was set up within these woods was done so some time in the sixteen-hundreds. Starting a settlement in a forest was not exactly the norm, so it's not clear why the people of this village chose to have their homes here. Of course, this unnamed village is not on any official record, so its existence has endured through folklore alone throughout the years. In fact, only last night we stayed at a place called Amaley, where a patron at the bar we were drinking at was all too aware of the lost village and the story that surrounds it. He even warned us off coming here, telling us it wasn't safe. Ominous words, indeed.'

Ken actually winked at the camera at this point, and Tony couldn't believe what he was seeing. His friend was displaying a hint of something Tony had never seen before: charisma. Perhaps James was finally getting through to him.

Ken went on, 'The story goes that the town flourished at first, the townsfolk making use of their immediate surroundings by constructing timber homes set into the large clearing they made. They traded with other local towns, including Amaley, for years, until things started to get weird. Stories began to spread to the nearby settlements of the strange things taking place in the village. Traders reported odd behaviour from its inhabitants. At first, the people became curt, then rude, and eventually aggressive. Formerly kind and generous people had changed. And, according to some, their appearance did as well, as the village-folk started to exhibit sunken eyes, gaunt flesh, and even teeth and eyes that didn't seem human—though whether this has just been embellished over the years is unknown. Then, a young man of no more than eighteen years of age turned up in Amaley. Weak, wounded, and close to death, he told tales of what was happening back in the village. A woman there, Mother Sibbett, had risen to prominence. She had convinced everyone in the town that their place was not to worship God, but something greater. Something more... real. The rudimentary church was transformed and used for rituals and acts that were definitely against God, in an attempt to insult and enrage him. There was sacrifice, blood-letting, and horrible sexual acts against man, woman, and beast. The young lad said the village collectively succumbed to a madness that had taken hold, and many of the village-folk were already dead, killed in an orgy of violence, orchestrated by the new elder. Fearing what was happening, the people of the surrounding towns agreed to cut the village off and never go back there. For over six years, they kept to their word and no one set foot in that forest, despite hearing strange and unexplainable things in the night emanating from the wooded area and carrying for miles around.

'And then, after hearing nothing from the village during all those years, a decision was reached. Search parties from the towns planned to venture into the forest to see what had become of their neighbours. Two parties were put together, one from Amaley and one from another local town, one that no longer exists today: Brumeer. The two parties then set out into the forest.

'The group from Amaley was gone for over a day, then returned to say they had found the village, or what remained of it. The place was abandoned. There were some human remains, but not enough to explain the disappearance of all those people. And what's more, the houses and structures were now black and decayed, like a sickness that had spread out from the church, the only stone building in the settlement. The blackness even travelled to the trees, pushing out for almost a mile in every direction. And that is how, supposedly, this forest got its name. The search party from Brumeer, however, was never heard from again.

'There are stories of many, many disappearances from the local towns over the years since—people going into those woods and never coming out again—but in more recent times, exploration of the Black Forest has shown no signs that a village ever existed. That might be understandable, given most of the structures were timber and could have, theoretically, rotted away, but the stories say the church was stone. And, unless it was specifically demolished, there should still be some sort of sign of its existence. And who knows, maybe this week we will find it.'

Ken then smiled. It was a rather theatrical, sinister grin. Then he looked to James.

'You done?' James asked.

'Yeah. I think that's enough.'

James nodded and shut the camera off. 'I was going to suggest talking about some of the disappearances, but I agree, that monologue was probably long enough on its own. We can pick up the other stuff later. Nice work.'

'Thanks. Think I'm starting to get the hang of it. So, what say we get some equipment set up and start our vigil? See if we can't get anything else on camera?'

Tony couldn't help but smile as well. The experience

from earlier had actually gotten to Ken, and in a really positive way. He was not the type of man to be easily convinced, and always focused on making sure any evidence they presented could hold up to the highest of scrutiny. Ken wanted, or needed, to be able to prove the things they investigated.

Now, perhaps Ken thought he'd struck the motherload.

It was certainly a nice change in the normally serious and gruff man, and Tony hoped the trip could continue its early success.

'I think we are going to get something tonight,' James said. 'I can feel it.'

7

————

ROBERTA HAD to admit that she hoped James' certainty the group would experience something during the vigil turned out to be misplaced.

She'd experienced enough for the time being and she was happy to let her exhaustion take over so she could sleep. Being terrified at things undead roaming outside of her tent was not something Roberta wanted.

Perhaps signing up for the trip had been a mistake.

Between them, the group had set up two cameras. The first was tied to the trunk of a tree, as high up as they dared fasten it, and gave a nice aerial shot of the campsite. The other was mounted on a tripod and faced out into the dark woods. Both had night-vision capability and, like most of the toys they had with them, were small and lightweight. Cumbersome equipment was not something they could afford to bring on an investigation like this, where an extended period of hiking was going to take place.

After a few hours of them thinking every little noise from the depths of the forest was something of significance, the group soon got used to the nocturnal sounds that turned out to be commonplace. As the cold grew deeper, boredom set in. The initial intensity of their concentration dropped along with the temperature, though Roberta kept casting glances around the camp, unable to shake the feeling they were being watched. It was probably just in her own head, and truth be told a certain paranoia had started to creep in ever since she'd entered the forest—since she thought she'd heard her own name whispered behind her—but she could see nothing out there in the dark.

The group began talking, hoping to fill the stretch of boredom and inactivity.

Roberta asked a little more about Ken's past, as he had always seemed like a private person. Other than anything company related, Roberta knew little about the man she worked with. He had a knack of avoiding questions, however, and put that skill to good use again.

'What about you, Roberta?' he asked. 'Italian roots, I'm guessing?'

Roberta nodded. 'My parents are Italian, and came over to England when I was three.'

'That explains why you don't have an accent,' Ken said.

'Do you speak any Italian?' Tony asked.

'I do.'

'Go on, then,' James said, smiling. 'Show them what you can do.'

Roberta chuckled, then took a breath. She spoke, taking on a natural Italian accent that she knew surprised both Ken and Tony. 'Sento che la follia é travolgente e non so cosa fare.' She was met with blank stares.

'I have no idea what you just said,' Tony replied.

Roberta laughed again, but there was a nervous twinge to it. As requested, she had given them a sentence in Italian, but was glad none of them had actually understood it.

The words she'd spoken had just come out, though she couldn't understand why, and that unnerved her.

'So?' James pressed. 'What did you say?'

'Learn to speak Italian and then you'll know,' she responded with a smirk, completely avoiding an answer.

'Tease,' James said.

'That I am. I'm also tired.' That wasn't a lie, but she was still confused at why she'd spoken that particular phrase to them. For now, however, Roberta just wanted to go back to her tent, away from these oppressive trees, and get some sleep. 'Sorry to cut the watch short,' she said, 'but I'm going to turn in. The rest of you feel free to stay up and wake me if you need to.'

'I'm not sure that's going to be necessary,' Ken said, checking his watch. 'It's approaching one in the morning. I think it might be a good idea if we all get some rest. We can leave the cameras running until they run out of juice, then see if we picked anything up when we review the footage. We've had a good day today, so let's get recharged and ready for tomorrow.'

Roberta was pleased to hear that, as it meant she didn't have to go back into the tent alone, though she expected James to argue and push for extending the vigil.

'Yeah, sounds like a good idea to me,' he said, getting to his feet and stretching his arms above his head.

And so it was settled. They all said their goodnights and entered their respective tents. In the dark of the nylon enclosure, Roberta and James fumbled about as they got into their sleeping bags.

'So I guess you aren't feeling particularly amorous?' James asked as Roberta felt his hand caress her face.

'Afraid not,' she replied. 'But I wouldn't mind a snuggle.'

James took the hint and shuffled over to her, letting

Roberta roll into him. He dropped an arm over her side and pulled her into a hug.

'Goodnight, baby,' he said and kissed the top of her head.

'Goodnight,' she replied. 'Sleep tight.'

It didn't take James long to drop off to sleep. She heard his breathing deepen when he did, and it bordered on a snore. It took Roberta longer to drift off, however.

She could not stop thinking about what she'd said earlier, completely involuntarily.

The madness overwhelms me and I don't know what to do.

Why the hell would she say that?

Roberta didn't know how long it took, but she eventually dropped off to sleep as well. Sadly, it was to be short-lived.

8

Tony's mind swam.

It was a confused mess caught partway between the odd dream he was experiencing and the waking world pulling him back, ruining his slumber. Horrible sounds came from all around him.

He sat up, and it took him a few moments of blinking in the dark to get his bearings.

Tony was in his tent, packed tightly into his sleeping bag, and the lack of light penetrating the covering meant it was still night. His body ached for more rest, but noises outside of his tent meant his mind was far too active for that now.

And far too afraid.

The sounds the group had heard earlier, in broad daylight, had seemingly returned... with a vengeance.

Ghoulish moans, cries, and screams of pain could be heard from all sides. And while they definitely seemed to be coming from a ways away, this time they were certainly not faint. They were clear, and there seemed to be multiple voices this time, too.

An icy chill gripped Tony, seizing his joints together and

rooting him to a seated position in the false safety of his tent.

What do I do?

Perhaps grabbing his camera and getting outside to record what was happening should have been the first thing to pop into his head, but it wasn't. Tony was scared, and his hands gripped the sleeping bag tightly as he pulled it up to his face. What he wanted to do, as ashamed as he was to admit it, was to scream for the others.

He didn't have to.

Instead, Tony heard a zip open up from a nearby tent. At first he wasn't sure which one, but after a moment's silence the answer came to him as Ken spoke.

'Are you guys awake?' His voice was a loud whisper.

'Yeah,' Tony croaked out.

'We are too,' he heard Roberta respond. Her voice was shaky.

'You hearing this?' Ken asked.

With the others clearly awake, Tony found a little more courage and zipped open his tent, then poked out his head.

The air was much colder outside the tent, immediately biting at the exposed skin on his face. The first thing Tony saw was the deep dark that swallowed up the trees in the middle distance onwards, hiding all but those closest to him, making it look like an expanse of nothingness. He suddenly felt very small and alone, like a single star lost in the vastness of a black cosmos. The pained shrieks, no longer muffled by the fabric of the tent, were louder outside as well, and they echoed through the air.

Turning his head a little to his left, Tony could see Ken kneeling outside of his tent, his boots already on and his eyes wide and alert. To Tony's right, completing the semi-circle of tents, the heads of James and Roberta poked through the opening of their unzipped entrance flap. Roberta, in particular, looked terrified.

'This can't be real,' she whispered. Tony struggled to make out the sound of her voice over the chorus of pain that seemed to surround them. 'It's insane.'

'So what the fuck do we do?' James asked. Even he seemed hesitant, his previous enthusiasm now dulled. They all looked to Ken, who pulled out his camera and flipped open the viewfinder. He reminded Tony of a cop in a bad T.V. show, cocking his gun and ready for action.

'We do what we came to do,' he said. 'We get this recorded. Audio and visual. Let's see if there's anything out there.'

'But what if it isn't what we came for?' Roberta asked.

'Meaning what?'

'Meaning, what if it's people making those awful sounds? I mean real, living people.'

'Can't be,' Ken said. 'Listen to it. There are too many voices. I refuse to believe that many local townsfolk are here in this forest with us.'

Tony tended to agree with Ken's line of thinking. To him, the haunting, incessant moans could be only one thing. He was certain this was a supernatural event.

However, the feeling that overcame him while in the presence of one was not excitement, as he had expected, but utter fear.

The noise was everywhere. Whatever was making it had to have been everywhere as well. It made Tony feel vulnerable and insignificant.

Ken flipped a switch on his camera and Tony, even from this distance, saw Ken's own face on the screen of the viewfinder. He was recording himself.

'We've just been woken up to the terrible noises you can

hear all around us. We have no idea what is making them, but they are coming from all directions, it seems. We are going to try and record what we can, but given the late hour and the lack of light, we can't risk moving away from the campsite to investigate further.'

Tony almost breathed a sigh of relief.

Ken switched the mode on his handheld camera again and aimed it off into the forest. He then looked at the others. 'Are you coming out?'

Tony, with some hesitation, slid on his boots and tied up the laces, pulling them tight. He dug around in his backpack and found his camera as well, then got out, stretching up to his full height and feeling infinitely more exposed, like a hundred pairs of eyes were watching him from the dark.

James and Roberta joined him as Tony walked and stood beside Ken. They huddled together, each with a camera pointing out into the night.

'Everyone film a different section of the forest,' Ken said. 'Roberta, can you get the audio recorder from earlier?'

'Already have it,' she answered, pulling the small device from her pocket with her free hand. She flicked it on with her thumb and held it aloft.

They stood together, shivering in the middle of the night as the howling and moaning continued. James repeated Roberta's earlier statement, 'This is insane.'

Tony set his camera to night vision and the trees and ground on his screen flooded with a green hue. He was able to see a little farther in that mode, but not by much. Slowly tracking the area in front of him, Tony stared intently at his screen, hoping and praying that nothing would show up and freak him out even further.

'Listen,' Ken said, tilting his head to the side like a dog.

Tony didn't want to, but soon understood what had caught their leader's attention.

The moans and cries were quieting, yet again slowly fading away.

'It's stopping,' James said. 'Like it did before.'

Less than a minute after they noticed the drop, the sound that had surrounded and terrified the group disappeared completely, leaving them all in silence. Not even the noises of nocturnal wildlife could be heard, only that of the wind and the swaying and creaking of branches.

It was James who eventually spoke. 'I can't believe that. Honestly. I just can't get my head around what we heard. It was everywhere. Fucking. Everywhere. Surely this is proof?'

'It's as close as we've ever gotten,' Ken replied.

'Let's just hope we picked it up again.' James started to fiddle with his camera to play back the recent footage, but was stopped when Roberta let out a piercing scream.

Jumping at the sudden sound, Tony whipped his head around and saw Roberta backpedaling and pointing out towards the trees, her eyes wide in panic.

'What is it?' James asked, dropping his camera and putting a protective arm around her. He cast his gaze out into the night, as did Tony, who could see nothing.

'I saw something,' Roberta spat out. 'A woman, standing out there. I saw her!'

'Are you sure?' Ken asked as he paced out ahead of them, showing little-to-no fear.

'Yes!' Roberta yelled. 'Ken, don't go out there.'

Ken stopped, still a distance from the rest of them, and scanned the surrounding area. His camera was switched to night-vision mode as well, to help him see anything that may be lurking in the dark. 'There's nothing here,' he said. 'What did she look like?'

'Horrible,' Roberta said and quickly moved back towards her tent. Her hands were wrapped around her own chest and tears started to form in her eyes. James stayed with her and pulled her in for a hug. 'She just looked... wrong.'

'Check your footage,' Ken ordered, but Roberta shook her head, clearly not wanting to see the strange woman again. Ken walked over and gently took her camera. 'It's okay,' he said. 'Let me see.'

Tony and James looked over Ken's shoulder at the camera's viewfinder. The footage was rewound and played again. It was unsteady, and on it they heard James talking, then Roberta's scream. The camera shook and dropped, then stayed pointed to the ground. But during all that, Tony could see nothing out of the ordinary.

Neither, it seemed, could Ken. 'Damn it.' He rewound and replayed it again. This time, he slowed the playback down and inched it forward frame by frame.

'I don't think I got it,' Roberta said. 'I was aiming the camera in a different direction. I just turned my head and saw her. I didn't even point it at her, because I panicked. But I saw her, I swear.'

Ken reviewed each frame anyway, but Roberta was right —there was no image of a woman in this footage—at least, not in the section they had just watched.

'We need to stay focused,' Ken said, his voice stern. 'If we think we see something, we need to get it. That should be our first priority.'

Roberta looked shocked and more than a little hurt. 'I'm sorry, Ken, but I was a little freaked out.'

'I understand,' Ken said, 'but that's why we're here. I keep saying it, but we need to put our fear aside. Nothing here can hurt us. I need everyone to be in their game, vigilant, and in the correct mindset.'

'Hey,' James snapped, stepping away from Roberta and towards Ken. 'The lady got scared, all right? It isn't her fault. Give her a break.'

Ken made to step towards James in retaliation, and Tony noted the man's jaw was clenched. However, Ken stopped mid-step.

He took a breath.

'Fine,' Ken said, then he turned to Roberta. 'I'm sorry. Just, with everything that's been happening, I'm keen to get something visual on record.'

The angry expression on Roberta's face softened a little, but did not disappear completely. She nodded. The apology seemed to have sufficed.

Another silence fell over them, this one awkward, and Tony again looked out into the dark forest wondering if Roberta had indeed seen a woman out there, or if perhaps her tired mind had been playing tricks on her.

'I wonder who the hell it was,' James mused.

'I know who it was,' Roberta said, stepping back into her tent and pulling off her boots. Before she disappeared inside completely, she added, 'It was Mother Sibbett.'

9

JAMES WAS WORRIED ABOUT ROBERTA.

She looked tired this morning. Hell, they all were, and James doubted anyone got much sleep considering the events of the previous night. But it was more than just that with Roberta... she seemed fragile and frayed at the edges.

And scared. Really scared.

After James had entered the tent with her the previous night, he had questioned how Roberta knew the mystery woman she had seen was Mother Sibbett. Roberta would only give one answer: I just know. And she would not talk about it any further.

That morning, sitting close to the campfire in silence as Ken and Tony tended to breakfast, Roberta looked pale, and her eyes appeared a little sunken with dark circles beneath. James was worried she might actually be ill, though she denied it, claiming she was fine, just tired.

Ken was cooking chicken and vegetable stew from a packet; he poured its dehydrated contents into a tin that was being heated over the fire, bubbling as it mixed with boiling water. Roberta's portion was served up first, and she gobbled it down in only a few mouthfuls. James ate next, then Ken and Tony turned their attention to preparing their own food. During this time, no one said much of anything.

The previous day's enthusiasm seemed to be heavily dampened after last night, which was a shame to James, as they should have been elated at what they'd gotten as evidence. Maybe they still could be.

Without a word to the others, James stood and walked back to his tent, leaving Roberta staring at the flames. He went back to his camera again, plugged in his headphones, and listen to some of the previous night's footage.

He smiled.

As with the faint voices that day, they had again picked up the mysterious sounds from the forest. Only this time, the chaotic din was much more urgent. The voices, just as he had remembered, were everywhere—cries of people in agony.

To James, there was no way it was anything other than paranormal. It had been scary when in the midst of it—even he had to admit that—and Ken acting like an arse hadn't helped matters at all, but regardless, they *had* something. Two major events in less than twenty-four hours. Those, as well as Roberta's sighting. James understood why Ken was disappointed they hadn't gotten that on camera—he was as well to a certain extent—but it wasn't fair to blame Roberta for being scared.

That being said, there was no reason to let any of this ruin the investigation, especially such a fruitful one, as they were just getting started, and had already garnered great results. If the recorded voices weren't enough on their own, there was still the chance they could catch something on this trip that would propel them to stardom, far beyond simple internet fame. Perhaps even an actual television show.

It was an exciting thought.

He left the tent and addressed the group. 'Okay, I know we're all a little frazzled and grouchy this morning.' The others turned to look at him. 'Last night was like nothing I've ever experienced before, and I can imagine that is the same for the rest of you. Our nerves were frayed, no doubt about that. But I think we need to remember that this forest is delivering.' He held his arms out wide, gesturing to the area around, then waved his camera. 'Just did a quick check. Happy to report, those voices we heard weren't just in our heads. We caught them on tape. More evidence, this time even better. There will be lots to review, but this is great stuff already. What we are getting here could change our fortunes. Literally. There is something about this place that, I don't know, seems like the real deal—the thing we've all been looking for. And I think we should keep that in mind and pick ourselves up.'

He hoped it was a rousing speech, but the faces that stared back at him seemed blank.

At first.

Finally, both Ken and Tony looked to each other, then back to James, and smiled. Roberta was looking at him too, but her expression was more unreadable.

'I think you make a lot of good points there, James,' Ken said.

'For sure,' Tony agreed. 'Think that may have been the shot in the arm that was dearly needed.'

James hoped Roberta would add to that, to show that she, too, was still eager to make the investigation a success. However, she stayed quiet.

'So,' James continued, 'perhaps we review some of the

footage from last night? I mean, spending another day hiking is an option, but why not take a minute see what we've got right here?'

Tony nodded. 'Makes sense.'

'But it can't be an in-depth review of the footage,' Ken warned. 'We only have a limited number of backup batteries, so I'd like to preserve as much power as we can.'

'Agreed,' James replied. 'So why don't we just look through the cameras we left running through the night? Maybe we caught something on one of those.'

They were all in agreement, even Roberta, though she was a little more hesitant.

Ken and Tony scanned the footage from the camera that had been positioned up in the tree, and James and Roberta went through the one that had been ground-mounted and aimed out into the night. Given there were hours' worth to wade through, both groups tried to quickly skim through what was available, fast-forwarding playback. Roberta still hadn't said much, but her gaze was fixed on the screen, just as James' was, and they both watched the green-hued footage zip through its runtime. The only way they knew that time was actually passing, was the quick swaying of branches in the wind. Other than that, all was still, and at first, it looked like all there was. A half hour's worth of footage passed, then an hour, then more still and James thought it was going to be a bust.

But then it happened.

'What the fuck,' James let out. He hit the stop button, then rewound the tape.

For some unknown reason, the night-vision mode had failed at one point, switching back to normal colours that were shrouded in dark, with the closest trees only barely visible. This switch of modes lasted only for a few minutes, and then flicked back.

James and Roberta reviewed it again, this time slowing it down to normal speed, watching the anomaly flick from green, then to full colour and then back again.

'Strange,' James said, looking at the screen, but he felt Roberta's eyes on him. He turned to her and saw a look of panic on her face. 'What's wrong?'

'Didn't you see her?' Roberta asked. By now, Ken and Tony had taken an interest and made their way over, standing above the squatting couple and looking at the camera from over their shoulders.

'See who?' James asked.

Roberta took charge of the camera and rewound it again before playing it back at a reduced speed.

They all watched.

'There,' Roberta said, pointing to the screen. Her finger was over one of the trees.

James saw it.

'Holy shit,' they heard Tony say from above.

James rewound the footage and watched again, focusing on that specific spot, the playback still slowed down. His breath caught in his throat as he saw a blurred figure become visible for a few moments. The unclear outline of a figure didn't step into view, but instead seemed to fade into existence, half of its form peeking out from behind the tree trunk.

'That's who I saw,' Roberta said, her voice little more than a timid whisper. 'Last night. That's Mother Sibbett.'

10

TONY LOWERED his head to the view-finder and squinted at the now-frozen image. He felt Ken doing the same beside him. A sense of anticipation rose from within as Tony tried to determine exactly what he was looking at—was it actually a figure, or something more explainable?

It didn't take him long to reach a conclusion.

Given that the camera had been in a fixed position during the night, and did not appear to be shaking due to excess wind, it was odd that the thing they were looking at, peeking out from behind the tree, was blurry. However, despite the rather distorted appearance, it was quite clear to see it was a human shape. There was a definite head, with long, thin black hair shaping a skeletal face. The mouth hung open, but the image wasn't clear enough to see into the void. Dark clothes, framing the body, blended into the night, losing much of their definition. At the waist, Tony could clearly see a hand with long fingers. Though the face was difficult to make out, there was a distinct yellow glint to the creepy eye staring back at them all.

Even with as much objectivity as he tried to muster,

Tony could only reach one conclusion—that this was indeed a person—and the sight of it chilled his blood. Tony felt an ominous threat pour from the still image on the screen and, somehow, he knew that Roberta was right.

Besides the ominous feeling that wormed up from his gut, there was a distinct excitement, too.

The sounds they had previously recorded had been one thing, but this was on another level. They had something genuine here that would get them noticed.

'I don't believe it,' Ken said and squatted down further. 'James, can you play that again? Real time, and then at a slower speed?'

James obliged.

In real time, it was trickier to see the mysterious figure fade into view. It was like one moment there was nothing, the next she was there—if it indeed was a she. And then, after less than a minute of watching the camera, it vanished. When slowed, frame by frame, it was more discernible to see the woman materialise and then fade away again.

'We have something real here, don't we?' James asked, almost giddy.

Ken gave him a hearty slap on the back. 'I think we do. I honestly think we do!'

The three men broke out into cheers and claps, James throwing a celebratory fist into the air. He and Ken shook hands, unable to hide their smiles.

'I don't believe it,' Ken said again. 'I just...' He shook his head, not able to find the words, but Tony understood.

'I know,' Tony told his friend. Tony knew how much it all meant to Ken, and why finding this kind of proof was so important.

And here it was. They'd done it.

'Do you think she was picked up on the other camera?'

James asked, pointing to the one that Tony and Ken had been reviewing.

Tony shook his head. 'I don't think so. We didn't see anything, and I don't think the shot picked up where she was standing.'

'But we still have that,' Ken said, pointing to the image frozen on the viewfinder.

'And we aren't even close to being done,' James said. 'Imagine what else we're going to capture this week. Hell, it's a success already, but there's more to come. When we get all of this uploaded, the internet is going to go crazy.'

Tony laughed. He knew that James might have a point, but for Ken, who had hold of the camera and was again staring at that unsettling image, it meant much, much more than just fame and accolades.

Tony looked down to Roberta, who was staring away, pale-faced—the only one not joining in with the celebrations. He knelt down next to her.

'You okay?' he asked quietly.

She gave a half-hearted smile and nodded. 'Yeah.' He didn't buy the answer for a second, but Roberta rose to her feet before he could respond. 'So what's the plan for the rest of the day?' she asked. 'Are we staying put or moving on?'

The other members of the group cast glances to each other, unsure of the answer. Ken rubbed at his beard as he considered their options.

'I think we move on,' he said. 'I mean, we came here looking for a lost village. Not that I think we will find it, but there is so much out there; it would be a shame to stay put here the whole time. We'll head out, if everyone agrees, of course. We all have a say.'

'That makes sense to me,' Tony said.

James nodded. 'I'm up for a little more hiking. But which way do we go?'

Ken smiled and pointed in the direction the camera that picked up the image had been facing. 'Well, if that really was Mother Sibbett, it appears she came from that way. Why don't we head in that direction and see what we find?'

And so, a plan was formed. They quickly got to work dismantling the camp, packing up their tents, and putting away all of the equipment. It took well over an hour, but finally, they were ready and made their way out.

As they started off, James whistled the tune of *Hi-Ho, Hi-Ho* from Snow White, drawing a laugh from Tony and Ken, and it only helped to keep up the levels of excitement. Tony was fatigued from the previous night, but that morning's discovery, while creepy, had energised him. And it seemed to have done the same for the others as well.

All except Roberta, who still hadn't said much.

She followed on with them, but showed no signs of enthusiasm. Tony knew that was a subject which needed broaching soon, as it was unfair to make her endure the rest of this trip if she was truly scared, but he decided to give her a little more time, planning to bring it up when they next stopped. It did mean going farther into the forest, of course, and that would entail more backtracking if things needed to be cut short, but he wanted to give Roberta every opportunity to snap out of it. If they did have to call things off after finding so much already, Tony knew that Roberta would end up regretting being the cause of it.

Or, perhaps the truth was that he just didn't want this to end, and was going to selfishly avoid raising the issue for as long as he could. Perhaps that was also why Roberta's boyfriend wasn't addressing the obvious, either.

They walked on for a few hours until Tony needed to

call a halt, feeling a pressure from his bladder that he could not ignore any longer.

'I'm going to need a toilet break,' he said, last in the single-file line they had adopted. With Ken in the front, the group had been making its way along a thin trail they had come upon. The quantity of trees had really started to thicken up now, indicating they were getting deeper and deeper into the forest's confines.

Ken stopped and turned. 'No problem,' he replied. 'Anyone else who needs to go, now is a good time.'

As it turned out, everyone else had much stronger control than Tony, who made his way off into the trees alone. 'Don't go too far,' James called. 'We don't want Mother Sibbett snatching you up when you're out of sight.'

Tony laughed. But, as stupid as it sounded, that thought had already occurred to him. He made sure he was out of view of the rest of them, particularly Roberta, but was no more than a hundred yards away, hidden behind the thick trunk of a tree. Close enough to call out if anything surprised him.

There, he began to relieve himself, feeling the pressure ease up immediately, and he had to actually stifle letting out a groan of approval. It was then he focused on the tree before him. In many ways, it was nondescript, other than being fairly thick, but on the face of the bark, just above his eye-line, Tony saw it: a patch of black, seeping out from a knot in the surface of the tree.

The stain—if that was the right word—was in such stark contrast to the rest of the tree, Tony was surprised he hadn't noticed it straight away.

It was about the size of a human head—though Tony was confused as to why *that* was the reference point which came to mind—and its outer edges were formed of tendrils that reached out farther into what was otherwise a healthy tree, indicating it looked more like some kind of disease than a burn mark or anything of that nature. He held out a finger, pushing it into the thick substance, and it reminded him of what had fallen onto Roberta earlier. Were the trees in this forest sick?

And then he felt something touch the back of his neck.

It was like a finger pressing into the skin at the nape, digging in its nail, and an intense cold spread out from that point. Tony froze, panicked, the only sound that of his urine splashing off the tree and onto the ground below. He didn't know whether to stay motionless or spin round and confront whatever was behind him.

Tony then heard the exhale of a breath, and even felt it on the side of his neck. A rank odour flowed with it, and a stinging pain spread out as the nail embedded itself into his skin. It was quickly yanked down, tearing at the flesh.

Tony cried out and clamped a hand over the nape of his neck. He instinctively spun around, only to be faced with... nothing.

No one was behind him, and there was only the forest to see. It was impossible for someone to have disappeared that quickly. Tony rubbed his hand on the back of his neck around the painful area and felt something wet. He pulled his hand away.

He realised straight away that the hand he'd smothered the pain with was the same one he'd touched the black liquid with, and it was still smeared on his fingers, but there something else on his palm as well.

Blood.

A small smear streaked the meat of his hand. Panic rose, and he suddenly realised he was still urinating, pissing all over himself as fear forced more of the liquid out. Tony quickly aimed the stream away as he finished, his heart beating as fast as he had ever known, and he felt like he needed to get back to the others, quickly.

'Hey!' Tony heard James shout. 'You fall down a hole or you still pissing like a racehorse?'

Tony quickly pulled up his trousers and looked around one last time.

Still nothing.

He turned again to the tree, back towards the black on its trunk, but that stain had vanished as well.

Tony waited no longer and ran back to the group.

11

'YOU OKAY?' James asked as he saw Tony hurrying back towards them. The man looked panicked and ran all the way back to the trail, and once he reached the group James noticed something else. 'Jesus, did you piss yourself?'

Tony looked down, then back up to the area he had just emerged from. 'Something happened,' he said, breathless.

That caught James' attention. Ken's too, it would seem.

'What?' Ken asked.

'I—' Tony began, but paused, looking confused and trying to find the words.

'Did you see something?' James asked.

Tony shook his head. 'No, not really. But I felt something. While I was... you know.'

'Pissing?'

'Yes, James, pissing. I noticed a black mark on the tree. And then I felt... something... press into the back of my neck.' He turned his head to show them. 'But when I turned around, no one was there.'

'What is that?' James asked. 'There is something black smeared over it.'

'And there's blood,' Roberta stated, and the three of them gathered around.

'Holy shit, there is,' James confirmed. 'Something cut you?'

'I think so,' Tony said. 'Is it bad?'

James looked closely at the wound. It was definitely noticeable, and still bleeding, but wasn't much more than a deep scratch a couple of inches long. 'Nothing serious, but that black shit seems to have gotten in to it,' he said. 'Certainly weird. Perhaps you caught yourself on a branch or something?'

'No,' Tony replied with certainty. 'That wasn't it.' He then rubbed at the wound again and winced. 'Can someone help me clean this up?'

James pulled out his water flask and poured a little on the cut. Using his sleeve, he wiped off the blood and black sludge. The wound was cleaner now, so James retrieved the first aid kit and applied a plaster to it, protecting it from the elements.

'Should be okay now,' he said. 'Does it hurt?'

'A little,' Tony said. 'And I was sure someone was standing behind me when it happened. I even felt their breath.'

'You're saying you've had a physical interaction with an entity?' Ken asked.

'I guess,' Tony said. 'At least, I think so.'

'That's amazing,' James added, but Roberta shook her head.

'No!' she said. 'It isn't. He's hurt.'

'It's a small cut,' Ken said. 'Do you feel okay, Tony?'

Tony nodded. 'I guess. A little shaken.'

'But fine otherwise?'

'Yes.'

'No,' Roberta shouted, stamping her foot. 'Don't ignore this. If what he's saying is true, then one of these things has hurt Tony. Even if it's only a little bit, it's a warning that we need to take seriously.' She took a breath. 'We need to leave this place.'

James felt a twinge of disappointment when Roberta uttered those words. He had been expecting and dreading them in equal measure. Roberta hadn't been herself ever since she'd claimed to have seen that woman in the trees last night—something they could now verify thanks to looking at the footage—and no longer shared the rest of the group's enthusiasm at what they were discovering. Instead, she had let fear take hold, which was understandable, and James felt a sense of protectiveness over his girlfriend because of it, but he didn't want such a productive investigation to be cut short.

He believed, now more than ever, that this trip could catapult them up to a new level and bring them success that they barely could have dreamed of. With the results already, things would change for them, but he didn't want to settle for that. He wanted everything the Black Forest had to offer.

And all the riches and recognition that would come with it.

'Well, let's not get ahead of ourselves,' James said. 'We aren't in any danger here.'

'How can you say that?' Roberta asked angrily. 'Are you so blind? We need to get out of here. We aren't wanted, so let's just take what we've got and go home.'

A silence hung over them and James looked at each member of the group individually. It was easy enough to read the expressions of Ken and Tony—who had himself just been through a scare; they wanted to stay, but didn't know how to give voice to that in the face of an adamant Roberta.

So James decided to do it instead, though he knew he risked her ire in doing so.

'Roberta,' he said gently. 'I understand what you're saying. I do. What is happening is bizarre and unexplainable and... scary. But this is what we do. I honestly think we stick it out a little longer and see what happens. If we feel there is a real and evident danger, then I agree, we need to pack it up. But for now, I think that would be a rash decision.'

He turned to the other two for backup, and they nodded meekly.

'I promise, Roberta,' Ken said. 'The first sign of any real trouble and we are done here.'

Roberta just shook her head. 'Fine,' she snapped, then folded her arms across her chest. Everyone was still looking at her when she shrugged and added, 'Well? Let's keep moving, then. I've said my bit. No point standing around if you won't listen to me.'

After a moment of uncertainty, Ken started moving forward, followed by Tony. When they were far enough away, Roberta leaned into James.

'Looks like your little speech did the trick,' she said. 'You're pretty good at that kind of thing. But I know something the rest of them don't—that you are completely full of shit.'

The venom with which she spoke surprised James, but he had no opportunity to answer back as Roberta quickly took off walking as well.

He sighed, then followed. But James was certain he was

right on this one. Overreacting was not a reason to throw away everything that was so damn close. He knew better, and soon enough he knew Roberta would see it too.

12

GIVEN the eventful start to the day, and even the previous night, perhaps Ken could have forgiven himself for expecting things to continue to happen at a quick pace.

That was not the case, however.

Though they had walked and searched for hours and hours, there was nothing that stood out as being strange or out of the ordinary. Worse, a little after lunchtime, a heavy rain set in, forcing them to stop and find as good a shelter as they could beneath the canopy of a large tree.

Now, night was getting closer, and they started setting up their second campsite of the trip. The rain had stopped, but the ground was wet, leaving them all muddy and dishevelled, and even a little grumpy.

Once supper was finished and the stove packed away, James asked the question they had all been thinking: 'Are we carrying out a vigil tonight?'

The response was muted at best, and it was Roberta who made her case the strongest. 'I'm not. Not tonight. I'm exhausted, wet, and fed up. I just want to get some sleep.'

'Yeah, sounds like a good idea to me,' Tony agreed. 'I

don't think we have the energy between us for a vigil.'

Though Ken knew James would be disappointed with the news, he could see the logic behind it.

So they took care of nature's calling—where no one was assaulted by an unseen presence this time—and said their goodnights before retiring to their respective tents.

Ken curled up in his sleeping bag and closed his eyes. The bag kept him warm enough, but he could still feel a cold chill on his face. However, given he was fairly experienced with camping, it was a sensation he truly did not mind.

Ken tried to quiet his mind and push all their current success from his thoughts. He didn't want to overthink things, instead preferring to take them as they came and not get ahead of himself, which he had become close to doing earlier after seeing the footage from the previous night.

It was promising stuff, certainly, but it still needed to be thoroughly scrutinised, and that could only be done in the environment of the editing room, not out in the forest where they were right in the thick of the excitement.

If he was to finally get the evidence he craved—evidence that proved beyond doubt there was an afterlife—then it had to be irrefutable. And this proof wasn't for other people, either. Not really. He wasn't doing it so his peers would laud his work.

Ken needed to know for himself. There had to be more than just this life.

There *had* to be.

The last thing he remembered before drifting off into a deep sleep was a light rain pitter-pattering down onto the roof of his tent.

～

KEN WAS in the Black Forest. It was night time. He sat on the wet ground, completely naked, with the sloppy mud seeping up around his buttocks. A blanket of rain descended, coating his shivering body.

He was utterly alone, and the sky above was completely black. Starless. It was as if someone had hidden it with a blank canvas that stretched on forever, trapping him underneath.

Ken didn't know what to do. He was lost and alone and scared.

Then he heard something that made him jump. Somebody off in the distance cried out. A short, sharp sound that cut to his core. He knew instinctively who it was. The voice was young, female, and clearly scared. It was someone in imminent danger.

Instantly, Ken was up onto his feet, sprinting through the forest towards the noise that could once again be heard. The trees around him were almost as black as the blank sky overhead, making traversing through them dangerous. But he could not afford to stop.

A cry for help sounded. The same voice again. Ken couldn't speak or shout back, and he wasn't sure why. He had no voice. The air burned in his lungs while he pushed on as hard as he could, ignoring the pain in his muscles.

Hold on, just hold on. Please. I'll save you.

But then the screaming started. Genuine, prolonged screams. The pained, terrified wailing of someone young in absolute agony.

In the throes of death.

No! No, no, no.

Ken was desperate and knew he was too late. Still, he pushed on... and ran right into a downed branch, the jagged edge puncturing his chest. Ken was moving fast enough that the thick, strong spike pierced through his entire body, emerging out of his back.

The screaming continued.

Ken could still make no sound; he could yell no words of comfort in response or even vocalise his own, tremendous pain.

He had failed. Slowly, he felt the life drain away from him.

Then, ahead, a figure made its way out of the dark. Thin and skeletal, with glinting yellow eyes. Scraggly black hair clung to its skull-like head. A haunting cackle emanated from it.

The sky above then erupted into life. Stars blinked into existence, swirling around, pulling into a point to form something like a cosmic eye that surveyed everything beneath.

What was this hell?

The figure before Ken continued to laugh as the landscape around him changed. Nightmarish pillars of cylindrical black—gargantuan things—thrust upwards and pierced the sky. Monstrous shrieks sounded all around him. The very ground beneath him seemed to seep a viscous red liquid.

This couldn't be real. It had to be a nightmare.

Finally, he was allowed to scream.

KEN'S EYES OPENED WIDE. Had his throat not been so dry, the scream lodged there would have erupted from his mouth.

Disoriented, he quickly sat up, confused at the light that seeped into his enclosed surroundings. Then the fog of sleep began to clear, and he remembered where he was: in his tent, clothed, and perfectly safe.

He let out a breath and felt a layer of sweat coat his body. Nightmares had been a recurring theme for Ken in recent years, but he had never had any so surreal and vivid as that one.

After he pulled himself round, Ken put on his boots and left his tent, breathing in the crisp morning air of the forest. He smelled the wet grass and mud. The ground beneath his feet was damp, but it was not the mud-bath it had been last night.

He stretched out his muscles and checked his watch. It was a little after seven, and Ken normally woke a few hours before that. Then he looked over to the other tents next to his own. James' and Roberta's larger tent was quiet, with no one moving within. All seemed normal there.

Tony's tent, however, was different.

The door was open. Not just unzipped, but ripped open completely—torn away, with the contents from within spilt out across the ground, as if the shelter itself had been gutted and its insides dragged out to be left on show.

Tony's sleeping bag, his pack, boots, and clothes were strewn about.

Ken's heart seized in his chest and panic hit him instantly. Something was wrong.

Running over to the tent quickly, he poked his head inside. Other than the ripped door and state of Tony's belongings, nothing looked out of the ordinary. Except that Tony was not there.

Ken stood back up and turned to the forest.

'Tony!' he yelled. After waiting a short time for a response which never came, he screamed it out again. 'Tony!'

Ken heard a voice from behind.

'What's going on?' It was James. Ken spun around and saw the younger man's head sticking out through the entrance to his shelter. James' black hair was a mess and he was squinting, trying to block out the natural morning light from his sleepy eyes. 'Where's Tony?'

'I don't know,' Ken said, panic evident in his voice. 'He's gone.'

13

'WHAT THE HELL do you mean, *gone*?' James asked, incredulous.

'Look at his tent,' Ken replied, motioning to the shelter. James immediately understood. The ripped door and the fact Tony's stuff was strewn about did indeed seem very wrong. A sense of urgency filled James as Ken began to scream his friend's name even louder, hoping to get a reply. James quickly threw on his boots and started to lace them up. As he was doing so, he felt Roberta grab his arm. When he looked to her, he saw terror in her wide eyes, and tears that were still fresh on her tired, dirty face, staining her cheeks.

'We need to leave here,' she said in a whisper.

James finished tying his boots. 'Hun,' he replied, 'we need to find out what's happened to Tony.'

'But—' Roberta started to say, though James didn't let her finish. Instead, he got out of the tent. He didn't fully understand what was going on, or where the hell Tony was, but he knew that time was of the essence here.

'Couldn't he have gone off to use the toilet again?' James

asked. Even as he said it, he knew that wouldn't explain the state of the tent.

Ken stopped yelling for a moment and cast James a look that made it clear the question was a stupid one. When he replied, it was instead to offer a plan of action.

'We need to go and look for him,' Ken said, speaking quickly. 'If he isn't responding, then he needs our help. We have to get to him, quickly.'

'Okay,' James agreed. 'But where do we look?'

Ken glanced around, frantic, clearly trying to come to an impossible decision. He then walked over to Tony's tent and inspected the ground around the entrance. 'Perhaps there are tracks or something.'

'Tracks?' James echoed, and followed Ken's lead, looking around as well. He hoped to find something that would offer some clue as to what happened, but felt woefully unfit for the job at hand. James knew marketing and media, not forensics and investigation. Ken, it seemed, was a little more in-tune with what they should be looking for.

'There,' he said, pointing to a flattened patch of grass outside of the tent. The blades fell outward, indicating to James that something heavy had been dragged across the ground away from the tent. He noticed Roberta's head hanging out of the door to their own shelter; she looked apprehensive, but made no move to come out and join them.

Ken and James followed the apparent drag marks a short distance to an area where the green and yellowed grass faded away, turning to muck and mud. Here, too, there was something to follow: indentations in the dark ground that appeared to James as if two parallel objects with some weight behind them had been pulled across the area, displacing the mud. Perhaps heel marks from a person being moved? These tracks, however, eventually disappeared completely. Despite searching extensively, neither man could find anything else after the drag marks had stopped.

'Jesus, this looks like someone took him,' James said, motioning to the marks they had found. 'Just pulled him right out of here.'

'But why do they stop?' Ken asked.

James shrugged. 'Maybe whoever took him lifted him up off the ground.'

'And why didn't they leave any tracks as well?'

James searched for an answer, but none was forthcoming. Again, he felt out of his depth.

'We go that way,' Ken said, pointing off in the direction the marks had been heading before they disappeared. 'It's our best guess.'

'No,' Roberta said from the tent. 'We can't just go running off into the woods. It isn't safe.'

There was something about her tone that troubled James. She wasn't just scared—her shaking voice sounded absolutely terrified, and he could see that she was on the verge of tears. He didn't get the chance to respond.

'We have no choice,' said Ken, raising his voice. 'We can't wait around and debate this. Let's go.'

'What about all our stuff?' James asked.

'Leave it!' Ken snapped. 'Let's hurry up.'

James nodded and turned to Roberta. 'Come on, hun, we need to move. Get your boots on.'

'I'm not going,' she said with a shake of her head, then disappeared back inside.

'Goddamnit,' James sighed before turning to Ken. 'Give me a minute.'

'We don't *have* a minute.'

'Well I'm not going to just leave her,' James insisted.

'Then don't,' Ken replied. 'Make sure she's okay. I'll be back as quickly as I can.'

'Ken, wait,' James called, but Ken was already on his way, marching from the campsite. Part of James wanted to follow, as sitting back and leaving their boss to go alone felt wrong... and dangerous. But he couldn't exactly leave his girlfriend behind either. James suddenly felt a pang of anger towards Roberta for putting him in this position.

Ken continued out between the trees, calling out Tony's name before breaking into a jog. James turned and moved back to the tent, dropping to his knees and leaning inside. Roberta had moved to the back and had her knees tucked up to her chin. She was crying now, her whole body shaking as she sobbed.

James felt immediate guilt for his earlier flash of anger. Could you really blame somebody for being scared at all that had occurred? After all, Roberta had warned them, insisting they needed to leave the forest before something happened.

And now, with Tony missing, something *had* happened, and it appeared her ominous premonition was proven right.

'Hey,' he said, softening his voice, before crawling forward to put a protective arm around her. The poor girl looked exhausted. 'It's going to be okay. We'll find Tony, and then we'll get out of here. Everything will be alright.'

Her crying just intensified. 'It won't,' she said, pulling at her hair as if some invisible bug were crawling through it. James tried to force her hands back down. 'It won't be alright,' she went on. 'We'll never find Tony.'

'We will,' James insisted, but Roberta spun her head round to look at him. Her wet, red eyes looked wild.

'We won't!' she screamed. 'Don't you understand? We'll never find him because *she* has him. She took him.'

'She?'

'You know who I'm talking about.'

'Roberta,' James said, trying to be gentle in his approach. 'We don't know what happened.'

'I know,' she replied, her voice cracking. 'I know, because I saw it.'

James paused, her words taking a moment to register. 'What do you mean?'

Roberta's sobbing increased, and it took her a minute before she was able to form the words. 'Last night. I woke up in the middle of the night and saw that... someone was opening our tent.' James felt his blood run cold, but Roberta went on. 'I saw her. She looked in here. I saw her face, James. Her horrible, inhuman face. Then she left. I didn't want to watch, but with the tent open I could see her from where I was. She moved over to Tony's tent...' Roberta then started bawling completely, screaming out the next words. 'She took him, James! I saw her take him!'

'Roberta,' James said, firmly, feeling panic grow. 'I need you to tell me everything you saw.'

14

————

ROBERTA HAD no idea what time it was when she woke during the night, but it was still pitch black outside, with no light coming in through the fabric of the tent.

She wasn't sure if it was the strange dream she'd been having that had woken her, or something else, but she was instantly wide awake with her body and mind on full alert. It didn't take her long, however, to pick up on a subtle sound from outside the tent that made her body go rigid.

At first, she couldn't be sure she had heard it correctly and tried to convince herself it was something else, something more natural. But then it came again, echoing from a far-off place.

A cackle.

It was a horrible, sinister sound that drifted through the air towards her. The laugh then came again, only this time it sounded much, much closer.

The final laugh she heard sounded like it was right outside the tent. Roberta wanted to scream, but the sound would not release from her throat, such was the fear that locked her body and vocal chords. She could do nothing but lie there and hug herself tighter from within the confines of her sleeping bag.

Roberta then heard a scratching sound, as if something was being dragged across the material of the tent. Looking up, she saw—even through the dark—a thin divot in the cloth, moving from one side of the tent to the other, towards the doorway. A fingernail, perhaps?

Roberta's heart was pounding in her chest. She listened intently, and her fear peaked when she was treated to an instantly recognisable sound: that of the zip to the door slowly being pulled open.

Frozen with fear, Roberta was unable to summon her limbs to move, or her voice to scream. She watched the zipper slowly move down, taking an agonising amount of time in its descent.

And then the entrance was pulled open, revealing something that threatened to snap Roberta's mind. The thing—an old, vile-looking woman—that poked its head inside smiled and locked its wild, yellow eyes with Roberta.

Though the horrible thing Roberta now stared at did indeed resemble a female, Roberta knew it could never really be called human. Not given the twisted and horrific features it possessed.

At that moment, Roberta was sure she was going to die.

And not only that, but she felt she would lose her very soul to this... witch. Instead, the thing slowly moved away, backing out of the tent completely, leaving the doorway open just enough that Roberta could see it as it turned and drifted over to a different tent.

Tony's.

The entrance to his shelter was quickly torn open in a

flurry of activity, and the thing she knew to be Mother Sibbett disappeared inside. Items were flung from the tent before it reappeared soon after, dragging Tony along with it.

Roberta locked her gaze with Tony's as he was being pulled from his enclosure, and his eyes were wide open and frozen in fear, but he did not move. His head was turned to the side and the rest of his body was seemingly trapped in some kind of paralysis. The pleading stare on his face was that of a doomed man, but even though he could not move, she could read his expression well enough.

Help me.

But Roberta could not. She couldn't move, scream, or even barely breathe, let alone run out to aid him. Whether it was her own fear that held her in place, or something more unnatural, Roberta could not be certain, but it didn't matter. Tony was lifted up off the ground and pulled off into the darkness without even a scream.

He would die soon, Roberta knew, and she did nothing about it. Instead, she spent the rest of the night focusing on that open doorway to her tent, unable to force herself to close it. She stayed that way until morning broke and she heard Ken calling Tony's name. Only after James woke and rushed outside to speak with Ken did she feel her body relax enough to finally move.

And she broke down sobbing.

AND THAT WAS the story she relayed.

Of course, Roberta had not told James everything. How could she tell her partner that a witch had spoken to her in the night when it had poked its head in through the tent? Or even explain the vile, disgusting things it said to her that had turned her stomach... but only to an extent. While Roberta listened to the hag talk—mouth not moving, but the words still coming—she was aware that a small part of her mind actually found what she heard... enticing.

And that part of her yearned to know more.

15

KEN PUSHED ON, marching through the rising undergrowth that seemed to be getting thicker the farther he went. The air was cool and crisp, with the early sun bright. Under different circumstances, it would have been a fine morning in a beautiful natural setting.

But things had taken a dire turn: Ken's friend of over five years was missing. Tony was not an irresponsible person, so there was no chance of it being some kind of immature prank. And he would not have wandered off to explore on his own without alerting the others—he just wasn't that type of person. Add to that the state of his belongings, plus the marks they had found outside of the tent, and everything pointed towards one explanation—the worst had come to pass.

Ken knew that there were dangers to spending a week in the woods, but he had always expected those dangers to be natural: bad weather, an injury picked up during the hike, or an illness.

Even taking into account what they did as a group, and the things they investigated, Ken had never expected anything like this. None of their prior cases had been even remotely dangerous.

Creepy, sure. But never dangerous.

He called out to Tony again, hoping and praying that his friend would answer. Hell, even if he was stuck somewhere or hurt, if he'd answer then at least Ken would know where he was and could go help him. However, if Tony had truly vanished, then what would they all do?

They couldn't exactly just leave. That was what Roberta seemed to want, Ken knew, but that surely would be condemning Tony to death. If they left here without him, Ken was certain they would never see him again.

'Tony!' he called out yet again. It was futile. The only answer that came was the sound of a flock of birds that flew overhead, spooked at his outburst. He wasn't sure how long he had been walking, but he was pushing hard and eventually started to feel a burning stitch develop in his sides. Ken was a fit man for his age, but moving at such a speed and over uneven terrain was hard work for him. He gave himself a moment and looked around.

Ken knew he had been walking in pretty much a straight line, so finding his way back to camp shouldn't be too difficult, but he wasn't sure exactly how long he had been walking. He checked his watch and saw that it was still early morning. He couldn't have been going for more than half an hour, but there was still no sign of his friend. Ken knew the sound of his calls would reverberate quite far in the forest, so if Tony was close enough to hear them, he was unable to reply.

That was a troubling thought. But no more troubling than the notion that his friend was not able to hear Ken at all.

Not wanting to stop for too long, he strode forward

again. He knew his walking was aimless, with no trail or clues to follow—which in and of itself was a stupid move, as he now risked getting cut off from the others altogether. And then Ken suddenly realised just how isolated he was. What was stopping whoever—or whatever—had taken Tony from doing the same to him now? So bullheaded had he been that the thought that he was putting himself in danger had not occurred to him. Or, if it had, it clearly hadn't registered hard enough.

For a moment he contemplated going back, but if he did that, then he would be accepting Tony as lost forever. That thought pushed him on, harder this time—eyes forward, scanning the landscape ahead. More forest, just like he'd seen elsewhere, and nothing of note. Ken swept his eyes to the left, seeing only more of the same, then the right, and again there was just more of the... *wait.*

It wasn't more of the same. Ken stopped in his tracks.

A few hundred metres off in the distance, a person watched him—totally motionless, as if frozen in time.

Though time had certainly taken its toll on the decayed body of the stranger.

Even at this distance, and with his heart in his mouth at the sudden and unexpected sight, Ken could make out some of the wretched details. The man's hiking clothing was stained with mould—though much of it had been torn away, leaving rotted flesh with a green and blue tinge below. Bones protruded through the skin, and Ken could see that one leg, where the trouser material had decayed, was little more than a dirty-white legbone. The head and face of the man were harder to make out at this distance, but Ken was sure one of the eyes was missing, and the other glinted a dull yellow. Even more sickeningly, however, was the man's stomach, which had been pulled open, allowing its stringy, rope-like intestines to hang down to the ground.

Ken could feel his heartbeat increase, pounding in his chest as the realisation of what he was seeing hit home.

'Jesus Christ,' Ken uttered, unable to help himself. He continued to stare at the thing for a long time and, whatever it was, it didn't move at all, yet was somehow able to stand upright on its own.

It occurred to Ken to grab his camera and get this on film as evidence, but as soon as the thought entered his head, he immediately cursed himself, realising quickly that in his haste to run after Tony he had left the damn camera back at camp. He then felt an instant wave of guilt for thinking of the investigation—of getting evidence—when his friend was missing. What was of primary importance here? It shouldn't have been worrying about gathering footage. After all, proving beyond all doubt that life after death existed was important to Ken, but was it more important than finding his friend?

The fact that he couldn't immediately answer the question honestly was troubling.

As was the thing up ahead that continued to stand and stare. Its head moved, ever so slightly, rotating to give the one good eye a better view of Ken.

It was a terrifying sight, to be sure. Had things not taken a more serious turn after they had all woken up that morning, this rotted man would have been an exciting—if unnerving—thing for them to witness. But now, given what had happened to Tony, the sight before Ken was a very ominous one indeed, and it filled him with dread.

On top of that, Ken had no idea what to actually do next. Were they both just to remain like this, in an unmoving standoff?

Running seemed an obvious option to him, and perhaps the one at the front of Ken's mind. But then, would the strange man give chase? And, if he did, could Ken realistically hope to outrun it?

The corpse—if that was the right word—looked frail, and about ready to fall to pieces. But that didn't mean much, considering that—by rights—the man should not have been able to stand. Hell, he should not even exist.

Then the standoff was broken and the stranger moved, turning slowly and shambling off into the depths of the forest, lurching like the decomposed zombie it resembled. Perhaps that's exactly what it was.

And then Ken understood what he had to do.

It was a stupid, insane, irresponsible, and fucking dangerous play—a course of action Ken would admonish anyone else for taking in the same circumstance. But he did it anyway because, somehow, Ken felt he knew the creature's intention—it wanted him to follow it.

Ken had no idea why, or what it wanted to show him. But he truly felt that it could lead him to Tony.

Or maybe his own death.

Still, if it led to confirmation of what he so desperately needed to know—about death and the afterlife—would death be such a bad thing?

Perhaps it would lead to the reunion that he craved above all else.

Due to its slow and deliberate pace, it was easy to keep up with the shuffling thing ahead. In fact, given the speed at which Ken had been moving, the journey could be considered leisurely. However, he was careful not to get too close. He followed for maybe ten minutes—noting a length of intestine dragging on the ground behind the thing as it shuffled forward. The walking corpse, surprisingly, didn't make a single sound the whole time it moved. Eventually, it disappeared from sight when it stepped behind a thick tree and did not appear again from the other side.

Ken paused.

Perhaps it was a trap. Was the decaying stranger now waiting behind that tree for him, ready to pounce and devour Ken's flesh when he got closer? Ken decided to use caution and slowly arced around the tree, putting plenty of room between himself and the trunk, so that he could eventually see behind it without being too close.

And he saw nothing on the other side.

His rotting guide had apparently finished leading Ken on this merry dance. However, Ken could see nothing to show for the trek. The only thing Ken could see was more trees, more grass, more muck, and more mud.

The same scenery he had seen everywhere else in the forest. The only thing perhaps out of the ordinary was a sharp decline that seemed to start not far past the tree, the land beyond dropping down out of sight.

Or, he thought, perhaps there was something to the tree itself. Maybe it had stopped here for a reason.

Carefully, Ken approached the thick trunk, leaves and twigs crunching beneath him as he walked, which were the only sounds in the area. Everything seemed too quiet at that moment, and the hairs on the back of Ken's arms stood on end.

What the hell are you doing?

Closing in, Ken noticed a black stain on the bark of the tree trunk, spreading out in tendrils like a disease. And, up above, he heard a definite creak.

Ken tilted his head up farther, and then he saw it, swaying above him.

Neck stuck in a noose, a body swayed gently back and forth in the light wind.

It took Ken no time at all to realise that it was the same corpse he had just been following. The body rotated as it dangled, letting Ken see its rotten and skeletal face more clearly. There was no yellow glint to the remaining eye this time, and its mouth hung open, flesh rotted away and leaving the bone and teeth exposed. Intestines hung down from the open stomach, almost brushing Ken's head, and the insides of the open flesh were black and purple.

Ken immediately took a step back.

His first thought, after getting over the initial shock, was that this corpse could have been one of the original inhabitants of the lost village—the place they had been searching for. But, if that had been the case, then given the hundreds of years that had passed, this body should have now been little more than a pile of bones on the ground. Its clothes were entirely out of time and place.

This thing above him, Ken understood, was a little more recent.

He took a closer look at what remained of its clothing, and what should have been immediately obvious to him suddenly registered—this was one of the missing hikers. And Ken had been led to it by the very spirit that used to inhabit it.

He had to wonder what horrible limbo this poor soul was now living in, and suddenly the idea of dying there in the forest did not seem so welcoming; notions of a reunion with his loved one were now seemingly an impossibility, given the purgatory that could await him here.

And what of Tony? Was this the eternity he would now live out?

A renewed sense of urgency took hold of Ken. Feeling

like time was running out, he knew that he had to find his friend, and quickly. But he still had no way of doing so.

He looked out ahead, to the drop in the ground. Was the old, hanging body really all the spirit had wanted to show Ken? Or was there something else here?

He paced forward, reaching the edge of the slope, and looked down its expanse. Upon seeing what lay below, he gasped.

Instantly, Ken knew he should go back for the others right away, despite time being against him. There was indeed a chance Tony was here, but Ken felt ill-prepared to search what he was seeing all on his own.

Because it seemed the shambling corpse had indeed wanted to show him one other thing.

Ken had found the lost village.

16

ROBERTA WAS NOT HOLDING up well.

All that she had experienced on the trip was now getting to her, and the disappearance of Tony was just the latest in a line of events that chipped away at her resolve. Thankfully, James now seemed more understanding of her position of wanting to leave, and finally saw reason enough for them to get the hell out of there once Ken had returned.

If only they had all listened to her sooner. She genuinely thought it was now too late.

Though the initial encounters they had witnessed had certainly been creepy, Roberta wasn't sure why they had scared her so much. Sure, whenever things happened in an investigation she was always prone to freaking out a little, but she still loved the process regardless. But here in this forest, things had been different. The fear seemed to peak right out of the gate and shake her to her core, affecting Roberta far more than it had the others, it seemed. But things had progressed, and her reservations about this place were proven correct.

However, there was something else that worried her, too.

Roberta seemed to be at odds with herself, unable to form a consistent internal consensus on what she should do. It was almost like there was another voice inside of her, another presence, messing with her thoughts and draining her will, constantly battling her.

Roberta wasn't sure when she'd first noticed it—perhaps after hearing the wailing voice for the first time—but it had only grown in intensity over the last day. And now, when things were at their quietest, it felt like a war was raging inside her head, one that her own psyche seemed to be losing.

'Here,' James said to Roberta, standing above her as she lay on the ground outside of her tent. She looked up and saw that he was offering her a flask of water. 'Drink something.'

At the mere mention of it, her body craved the water on offer. Her throat felt as dry as sandpaper and the thought of the liquid cooling her gullet was a welcome one. Even so, her first instinct, for reasons she couldn't explain, was to reject the offer. She didn't want to accept anything from him.

Roberta had to catch herself, knowing how thirsty she actually was, and begrudgingly accepted.

'Thanks,' she said, not meaning it, and took the flask before pulling in long mouthfuls. The water was slightly warm, but still refreshing.

'Ken should be back soon,' James said, though his tone sounded more like he was trying to convince himself than state a fact.

'If he isn't dead already,' Roberta stated, coldly.

'He isn't. I know he isn't. We just need to be patient.'

'What we need is to get out of here. Ken didn't listen and ran off—'

'He went after Tony,' James interrupted.

'He doesn't know where Tony is!' Roberta snapped. 'None of us do. So he ran off without knowing where to look. It's his own fault. That doesn't mean we need to stay here and share the same fate.'

'We need to give him more time. He's only been gone a little over an hour. And besides, can you honestly say you could find your way out of here without him? Because I'm pretty sure I couldn't.'

'It can't be that hard,' Roberta argued. 'We just go back that way.' She pointed back behind the tents. 'It was pretty much a straight line, wasn't it?'

James shrugged. 'I don't know. And even if it was, we wouldn't get out of here before dark, so we would need to camp again. We aren't getting clear of the forest anytime soon, anyway, and we've been pretty reliant on Ken so far. We need to wait.'

'It was a mistake relying on him so much,' Roberta said.

'Perhaps. But it is what it is. So can we just wait a little longer before we decide to leave our friends behind?'

Roberta was silent for a moment, before finally uttering the words she had been trying to hold in, 'They aren't my friends.'

She could see from James' expression that her remark had shocked him. Part of her revelled in that. But at the same time, part of her felt eternally ashamed, as it simply wasn't true.

So why had she said it?

Roberta's thoughts ran back to the phrase in Italian that she had spoken the previous day, the one that had exited her mouth before she'd had a chance to even consider it. The one about an overwhelming madness.

What the hell is happening to me?

She expected James to say something back to her, to

admonish her—which she actually wanted—but instead he shook his head and walked away. He squatted near the rudimentary firepit they had used last night and tried to get it going again. There was no real point to that, as it wasn't very cold at the moment, but perhaps it gave him something to do.

The two of them stayed like that for a long while, in total silence, each in their own space. James successfully got the fire going and Roberta just looked on, wrestling with feelings of both spite and embarrassment.

Their standoff was only broken when James quickly lifted his head, like a dog on alert. Roberta looked up, in the same direction, and saw it too: a figure ambling towards them from between the trees. It was still quite a distance away, but Roberta felt another chill, uncertain of who—or what—it was. It took her a moment to recognise the walk.

It was Ken.

He waved over to them.

Roberta stood up, actually happy to see him after being so sure something had happened. Now, hopefully, they could get out of this place.

But then she noted that Ken was alone, and there was no sign of Tony at all.

Even so, Roberta hoped that maybe now they could all concentrate on getting the hell out of the Black Forest, back to civilisation, and let someone else search for their missing colleague. Someone more qualified, who actually knew what they were doing.

James called over to Ken as the older man continued his approach. 'No sign of Tony, then?'

Roberta could see a shake of his head before Ken replied. He seemed out of breath. 'Not yet. But I did find something.'

Roberta stood and moved next to James, and they waited for Ken to join them. When he did, she could see a sheen of sweat on his brow as he breathed heavily.

'Did something happen?' James asked. 'Have you been running?'

Ken nodded his head. 'A bit. I got back here as quickly as I could.'

'So what is it?' Roberta asked. 'What did you find?'

'Well,' Ken started. 'If you can believe it, I found the body of one of the missing hikers.'

Roberta let out a gasp. James, instead, verbalised his shock. 'Jesus Christ! Where?'

Ken pointed back behind himself. 'Out there, a ways from here. The body was hanging from a tree. It was decayed quite badly and... well... not in a good state, let's just say. But I don't think his death was suicide.'

As far as Roberta was concerned, it was just more justification for them to leave. What more would it take for this man to see sense? She was about to give voice to her thought, but Ken went on.

'There was something else, too, near the body. I found something. Something big.'

'What?' James asked.

'The village. The lost village of the Black Forest. I'm sure of it.'

Both Roberta and James were, again, gobsmacked, and it took James a moment to ask the obvious question, 'Are you sure?'

'I'm sure,' Ken replied. 'It was at the bottom of a sharp decline and tucked away. But there is no doubt. I saw over ten buildings—all basic and made of wood. And at the centre of it all was a small, stone church. All of the buildings looked quite dilapidated, and the forest seems to have grown considerably around them over the years, almost swallowing the buildings up. But they are there.'

James shook his head. 'That makes no sense.'

'How so?' Ken asked with a frown.

'Wooden buildings?' James asked. 'Still standing after, what, four hundred years or so? That can't be right. Surely they would have just rotted away by now. On top of that, I can't believe no one else has found it after all these years if it was so obvious.'

'What are you saying, James? Do you think I'm lying?'

'No,' James replied quickly. 'Not at all.'

'Then why are you questioning me? I didn't imagine this.'

'I'm not saying you are, Ken. But I thought the best we would have found of that village, if anything, would have been rubble or some vague evidence of a settlement. But finding the whole thing still standing? Something is wrong with that.'

Roberta was pleased James was now on the same page as her. If Ken had truly found what he claimed, then Roberta was sure it wasn't merely a collection of old, empty dwellings. There had to be more to it, because James was right—it *shouldn't* still be standing.

And yet, Roberta felt an unexplainable pull to go there, which was completely at odds with her desire to flee.

In college, Roberta had learned of Freud's life-and-death drives, which were different sides to a dichotomy within oneself. One instinct pushed towards safer, life-preserving measures. The other, darker drive encouraged dangerous and destructive patterns and actions.

The balance between the two was different in each person and could change depending on one's circumstance. So she had to wonder if this sudden need to see the village was explainable in such a way, especially considering how she had been feeling recently.

Had the whole ordeal really affected her mental state to such an extent?

Or was there something else drawing her to danger? Something more... sinister. The same thing in Roberta's head that had uttered the phrase yesterday.

The madness overwhelms me and I don't know what to do.

Because the desire to see that village was undeniably strong.

And, thinking about it logically, could there really be any danger? If that place was indeed what Ken said, then it was merely a collection of old houses. And seeing the village was the very reason they were here.

Roberta suddenly had to catch herself. *What am I thinking?*

She rubbed at her face, scratching at an itch that bloomed on her cheek, and she felt her fingernails actually puncture the skin.

How could she really think that going out there was in any way a good idea? The idea that Roberta couldn't trust her own thoughts anymore popped into her head.

'Well,' Ken began. 'It's there, just how I described it. And, more so, I think that's where Tony is.'

'How do you know?' James asked.

'I just do. And we need to go find him.'

Roberta saw a look of realisation dawn over James' face. 'Jesus, Ken, are you going to ask what I think you are? Think it through. That sounds stupidly dangerous, especially considering what we've already experienced.'

'We can't leave him, James,' Ken insisted. 'If you were stuck out there on your own, wouldn't you want us to try and help, rather than running away and leaving you to die?'

'He might already be dead,' James said. 'I know it's a harsh thought, but we have to accept it as a possibility.' James then sighed before going on. 'Besides, Roberta saw something else last night.'

'What?' Ken asked, casting a look to Roberta. James looked to her as well, prompting her to explain the situation, but Roberta had no desire to recount the tale.

So, instead, James spoke up. 'She said she saw someone pulling Tony from his tent.'

'What?!' Ken was incredulous. 'What the hell are you talking about?'

'She said it was a woman. Just dragged Tony along behind her. He was awake, but Roberta said he didn't do anything to fight back, like he was in a trance.'

'And then what?'

'She took him,' James stated. 'Dragged him off into the woods.'

'And you didn't think to stop her?' Ken snapped, looking to Roberta. His face reddened as his voice rose. 'Why didn't you alert the rest of us?!'

'Hey,' James said, stepping in front of Ken and putting a palm to his chest. 'She was scared and didn't know what to do. Don't get angry at her.'

'Angry?' Ken seethed. 'What else do you expect? We could have helped him, James. We could have stopped him from being taken.'

'I'm not so sure we could have,' James replied. 'Something very fucking wrong is happening here, Ken. And I don't think we would have been able to stop it at all. So please, just calm the fuck down. We need to think, not lose our heads.'

Ken was silent for a long while, breathing heavily, his

face still red. Eventually, however, he seemed to calm. 'We need to find him,' he said. 'And I think he's at that village.'

'You can't know that.'

'No, but it's as good a place as any to look.'

'Don't ask us to do this, Ken. Please,' James said.

'I *am* going to ask that, James. If you say no, then fine, you can go back without me. But, to be honest, I need your help with this. Tony needs your help, too. I need you to come and search that place with me.'

Roberta and James looked to each other, and for a few moments—that seemed like an eternity—they stayed silent.

It was Roberta who spoke first.

'We should go.'

17

JAMES WASN'T sure if he'd heard Roberta correctly.

Had she just suggested they push farther into the forest in order to find Tony?

Considering her previous aversion to staying in the forest at all, this came as something of a surprise. Especially after what she'd said about Ken and Tony, and just what they meant to her. Though, considering her erratic behaviour recently, should anything really be a surprise?

'Wait,' James said, shaking his head in confusion. 'You *want* to go and look for him? And you *want* to go to that place? A place, by the way, that shouldn't even be there.'

Roberta, still looking pale and gaunt—and sporting a scratch on her left cheek that James hadn't noticed before—sighed. 'I don't *want* to be here at all. But maybe Ken is right. If Tony is there, then we should go back and look for him. If we find him, we can finally get the hell out of here. If we don't, then we still get the hell out of here, but at least we tried. Does that sound fair?'

Roberta looked to James first, then Ken.

Ken seemed to be studying her face, clearly as surprised

at her attitude change as James was, but he quickly nodded. 'Yes,' he said. 'That's fair. If he isn't in that village, then I don't know where he could be. We aren't going to do any good if we all get lost in here.'

Roberta then turned to James. 'What about you? Do you agree as well?'

Her tone sounded like a challenge, a far cry from the whimpering, scared person she had been during their trip so far. She didn't seem herself, and it concerned James. But he did have to agree with her, as what she'd said made sense. 'Yeah, I'm okay with that.'

Roberta then focused her attention back on Ken. 'How far is it?'

'About a half-hour walk or so. Not too far.'

'And what do we do with our stuff?' James asked, motioning to the campsite. 'Pack it up and bring it with us?'

'I think we leave it as it is for now,' Ken said. 'We have to come back this direction anyway, whether we find Tony or not. We can pack up everything we will need when we get back.'

That made sense to James, but he did not think they should travel completely empty-handed. 'But we'll definitely need to take a few things. The first aid kit, as well as food and water, just in case. Better to be prepared. But other than that, we can travel light.'

'Agreed,' Ken said. 'Let's get some stuff together, and then we can head out.'

They then all went to their respective tents and gathered together only what they would need for the short trip. James had been feeling pangs of hunger all morning, but he knew there was no time to prepare a meal of any kind, so he made sure to grab a handful of chocolate bars and nuts—food that he could devour on the go to help keep his strength up. Next to him, Roberta quickly sorted her gear and climbed outside without saying a word, leaving James to finish up on his own. As he was pulling together the last of what he needed, he accidentally nudged the camera that had been in his pack and looked down to it.

He was quite aware that the investigation was now over, and the group was in an emergency situation. But did that mean *all* of the equipment should be left behind? For one, that would mean all they had found so far would be potentially lost forever, even if Tony was found alive and well. Second, if they did see anything else, then it would not get recorded in any way.

James struggled with the conflict. Would it be crass and uncaring to take the small camera? It was light and wouldn't get in the way, but then why should he even consider it if all they should be concerned about was getting Tony and then leaving this place behind.

Was *his* investigation really over?

James realised that he still couldn't ignore the magnitude of what they'd found so far—the evidence they already had—and what that could mean. Even if the worst had befallen Tony, they could still salvage something here, something that would make their whole expedition worthwhile.

James slipped on his pack, glad that it felt much lighter now, but also grabbed the camera as well.

Fuck it.

As he exited the tent, he saw Ken emerging from his shelter at the same time... camera in hand as well.

The two men shared a guilty look.

Roberta walked over and joined them. 'You really think those are necessary?' she asked, motioning to the cameras the two men held.

James wasn't sure of what to say. Evidently, neither was Ken, and they both stayed silent.

'Let's just go,' Roberta said. 'Hopefully, we can be back here in a couple of hours, and then concentrate on getting out.'

Ken took the lead as they marched out through the trees, again adopting a single-file line, one that felt unfinished now that they were a man down.

'Hey,' James said to Roberta, who occupied the centre spot in their line. He had spoken quietly enough that only she could hear. Roberta turned her head.

'What?' she asked, her tone curt.

'I wanted to check to see how you are.'

'I'm fine,' she said, though she clearly wasn't.

James had learned in life that when a woman told you they were *fine*, the next thing out your mouth had to be really well thought out. Unfortunately, what came out of James' was not.

'Well you don't seem fine,' he snapped back, tired of being spoken to like a dog.

She glared at him with a hate fuelled by hell itself. 'Oh, I'm *sorry*,' she shouted while stopping in her tracks. Ken stopped too, his head whipping around in surprise at the outburst. Roberta then launched into a tirade. 'Am I making this shit-show of a trip unbearable for you? Have things gone to shit? Why, if only someone among us would have had the good sense to point out that we should have left this place a long time ago, then maybe all of this could have been avoided. Oh wait, that's right, *someone* did.' She then marched over to James and slapped him hard across the face. The blow stung his cheek. 'Me!' she screamed. 'I *said* this was a mistake. I said we weren't wanted here, but no, you boys knew better, didn't you? Well, now look at the mess we're in. Tony's gone, and any one of us could be next. So no, James, I'm not fucking okay. But I'm doing the best I can.' She then struck him again, and again, lashing out in rage. James held his hands up to deflect the slaps as they came in, not wanting to retaliate, but at the same time feeling overwhelmed at the aggression she was showing. 'You always think you know better,' she said and began to cry, but she kept going, releasing a wave of pent-up anger. 'Well, you've probably killed us all.'

The blows stopped as Ken grabbed Roberta around the waist and pulled her back. The girl writhed and kicked in his strong grasp, almost slipping free.

'It's okay,' Ken said, restraining her, though without using any excessive force. 'It's okay, Roberta.' His tone was soothing. Eventually, Roberta stopped fighting, but the look that she gave James was like that of a savage, wild animal, teeth bared and eyes wide. Tears streaked her gaunt face.

'Fuck you, James,' she snarled through gritted teeth, before spitting in his direction. It didn't connect, but it didn't need to. The act itself was enough. James took two steps back, feeling shocked.

But that was not all. A huge wave of guilt and shame washed over him when he realised that every accusation Roberta had hurled at him had been absolutely true.

The girl shook off Ken's relaxing bear-hug, cast James one last hate-filled glare, then turned around. 'Let's go,' she commanded, walking off ahead.

James and Ken were left looking at each other, neither knowing what to say. James could feel his cheeks burning red, both from the force of Roberta's strikes and also from sheer embarrassment. 'We better go on,' he whispered to Ken. 'She doesn't know the way, so head up and take the lead again.'

Ken nodded and set off. James again took up his place last in line, but made sure to give Roberta plenty of space as they walked.

During the trek, he thought long and hard about what she had said. In doing so, he hated himself a little more, and for the remainder of the journey no one said a word—a sour silence befalling them all. Time passed slowly for James, and it seemed like an eternity before they reached their destination. But, eventually, they did. Ken stopped them and pointed off to a thick tree farther ahead. Beyond it, James could definitely see the start of a drop in the ground.

'Over there,' Ken said. 'That's the tree where I found the hanging body. It's on the other side. And down that slope is the village.'

James looked to Roberta, waiting on her reaction, but she didn't give one.

Ken slowly walked forward. 'Prepare yourselves,' he said. 'This isn't a pretty sight.'

Both James and Roberta followed him to the other side of the tree, and then they looked up.

There was no sign of a body.

18

A CONFUSED FROWN crossed Ken's brow. There was no body, no noose... no nothing.

'This can't be right,' he said in a voice laced with confusion and annoyance. 'The body was here. I saw it. I was led to it, for God's sake.'

'What do you mean, *led to it?*' James asked.

Ken barely heard the question, his mind racing to make sense of it all. He was certain the shambling corpse he'd followed had wanted him to find that hanging body in the tree. So where the hell was it?

'Ken,' James said, louder this time, pulling Ken back from his thoughts. 'What do you mean you were led to the body? What led you to it?'

Ken hesitated, trying to figure out how best to answer the question. Back at the camp, when telling James and Roberta what he'd found, Ken had been close to divulging the story of the thing he had seen—what he'd assumed to be a spirit—and how it had led him to that very spot. But, as he was talking about the village at the bottom of the slope, he realised that if he wanted their help in searching the village, then telling the other two about his decaying guide would not help his case. Certainly not with Roberta. So he had made a quick decision and not divulged everything.

It was a selfish thing to do, and certainly underhanded, but he had acted out of instinct.

And fear.

Because, truth be told, the very reason he hadn't run down to that village and searched for Tony the second he'd laid eyes on it was because the sight of the place filled him with an apprehension and dread he had not felt before in his life.

Whatever intuition was telling him that Tony was in that village also told him that searching it would not be safe. Certainly not alone.

'Ken!' James shouted, annoyed at being ignored.

Ken hung his head, knowing there was no way of avoiding it now. He would have to come clean and tell them what he should have right from the start.

'I... saw something,' he eventually said. 'When I was looking for Tony. It was a figure, standing off in the distance. Watching me.'

'Mother Sibbett!' Roberta exclaimed.

'No,' Ken quickly replied. 'No, it was male, I'm sure of it. Though it was hard to be certain.'

'And why was that?' James asked.

'Well, I know how this is going to sound, but the figure was... kind of decayed.'

'*Kind of decayed?*' James asked, shaking his head. His tone was confrontational. 'Do you want to clarify that a little?'

'It's just what it sounds like—the man's flesh had rotted away. And his stomach had been pulled open. He looked like a standing corpse. For the longest time, we just stood and stared at each other, but then he turned and walked away. I don't know why, but I followed him.'

'I can't believe I'm hearing this,' James said, letting out a laugh of disdain. 'You're telling us you followed a fucking zombie?'

'As I said, I know how it sounds. I'm certain it was a ghost or spirit of some kind, and it wanted to show me something. It led me to this tree, then disappeared behind it. When I looked up, I saw the same body swinging from a noose. And there was a black mark on the tree as well...'

Ken trailed off as he looked at the bark, seeing no sign of the previous dark stain.

'And that's gone, too?' Roberta asked, though it was more a statement than a question.

'It would seem so.'

'I feel like I've been saying this a lot,' James said, 'but that is insane.'

'I'm telling you what I saw!' Ken shot back. 'I'm not making this up.'

'See, that is the insane thing about it all,' James replied. 'I believe you. I believe you saw an entity of some kind. I believe it brought you here. And I believe you saw a body up there,' he pointed to the branches above, 'swinging by its neck. I also believe you when you say there was a village down there.' Now he pointed to the head of the slope. 'I believe all of it, Ken. What I'm worried about is that you willfully followed whatever the hell it was. That was stupid. And going down to that village, if it's even there, could be just as dangerous.'

'But Tony *is* down there,' Ken said. 'I just know it.'

'You know it?' James asked, shaking his head. 'And somehow you knew that entity wanted you to follow it. And

Roberta here *knew* the old woman she saw in the woods was Mother Sibbett.'

'What's your point?' Roberta asked.

'My point is, these intuitions we seem to be having are pretty strange, don't you think? We seem to *know* an awful lot, without actually learning anything. Are we really coming to these conclusions on our own, or is there something else at work putting the ideas in our heads?'

Ken gave pause and considered James' words. Did the young man have a point? Were they all being toyed with by some unknown force that had taken up residence inside their minds?

If that was the case, could Ken be sure that his thoughts were even his own anymore?

James then slowly moved away from them. 'Where are you going?' Roberta asked as the young man walked towards the decline.

'To see,' he stated. 'See if this village is still there, or if we are just being fucked with, as I suspect.'

Both Ken and Roberta remained silent as James reached the edge of flat ground and looked down. He remained silent.

'Well?' Ken asked.

James turned round to face them and shook his head. 'Nothing.'

19

'THAT CAN'T BE,' Ken said, shaking his head in disbelief.

James looked down the slope again to the ground below. He saw trees, shrubs, and a lot of mud, but certainly no buildings. Ken jogged over to join him and looked down as well, and James registered a look of confusion and disappointment on his colleague's face. The bearded man's body seemed to deflate and his shoulders sagged.

'I just don't understand it,' he said.

James put a hand on his shoulder and gave it a friendly squeeze. 'I don't doubt that you saw it, Ken,' James said. 'But we just don't know *what* exactly it is you saw.'

Ken's head rose back up and his brow creased. 'Maybe this is where the town once stood. Maybe that's what I was being shown. And perhaps we can find some evidence of it down there.'

James paused. 'Evidence? I thought we were looking for Tony.'

'And he could still be down there,' Ken said with a sense of urgency. 'We need to go and check.'

James gave a firm shake of his head. 'Hold up, Ken. The

idea was to look for Tony in the village you discovered. We said that if we couldn't find him, we were going to leave. There is nothing down there—you can see that yourself. So, that being the case, shouldn't we be getting the hell out of here?'

Part of him wanted to stay and search below, of course, to see if they could find evidence of this fabled lost village and their friend, but he knew Roberta needed to get out of here for her own sanity. And his overriding drive now—especially after the tongue-lashing she had given him earlier—was to get her out of danger. He turned to her and asked, 'Do you agree?'

Roberta stared at them both and gave an exasperated sigh, like a tired mother caring for two unruly children. 'Let's go down and see what we can find. But we make it quick.' James was stunned at what she said, and even more so when she started down the decline, side-stepping steadily, using one hand for balance and the other to cling to reeds, vines, and clumps of grass on the slope as she descended.

Where was her urgent need to get out of the forest now?

'I don't get her,' James said under his breath so that only Ken could hear. 'Does she want to get out of this place or not?'

Ken shrugged and smiled meekly. 'Well, let's be quick, like she says. If there really is nothing down there, we'll soon know.'

James gave up, not sure what he was supposed to do anymore. He nodded, and the two men then followed Roberta, moving carefully down the hill and clinging on to the ground to ensure they didn't tumble and fall. It occurred to James as Roberta reached the bottom—with them not far behind—that if they needed to get back up this steep bank quickly, climbing it would not be an easy task. Especially considering the slick condition of the muddy ground.

Once he and Ken reached the base, they all began walking farther out into the area before them, searching for signs of, well, anything. The trees down there were not as densely packed together as elsewhere in the forest, and the ground was covered with long, knee-high grass. James could actually picture small buildings existing in that area, given the room, but it still wouldn't have been a natural setting for a village, and the structures would have to have been wedged between trees. But still, out of all the places they had seen so far, this was the most likely to have been the site of the settlement all those years ago. Roberta walked off farther ahead, searching the area of long grass, kicking through it while keeping her attention focused on the ground.

Where is that fear now? James thought.

Not too long ago, she had been terrified of her own shadow. Not anymore, it seemed. Hell, she had even screamed at him, belittled him, and struck him. Now she just waltzed off ahead without a care in the world. He debated shouting over to her to tell her to stay close, but remembered what had happened the last time he'd dared say something that Roberta didn't like.

So he remained silent and searched the area himself, scouring the ground. The group fanned out as they moved ahead, unsure of exactly what they expected to find. James had a horrible feeling that they might actually stumble upon Tony down here, but not as they wanted. Images of coming across his corpse in the long grass, milky eyes staring skyward, played through his mind.

However, in the half hour of searching, they found no

body and no trace of Tony at all. And no signs of any former settlement.

'Okay,' James called out, kicking out at some weeds in frustration. 'I don't think we're going to find anything here. I say we call it and head back.'

There was a silence from the other two, with Ken in particular looking uncomfortable. 'So are we just leaving Tony, then?'

'He isn't here, Ken,' James said with a raised voice. 'That was the plan. If we couldn't find him, we go.'

Ken let out a sigh, but nodded his consent. 'You're right,' he replied, and cast another futile look around. 'Let's go.'

First, they carefully made their way back up the hill, with Ken falling once as they went. But he managed to hang on, and stopped himself slipping all the way back down to the bottom. From there, they had the long walk back to camp. James noticed that Ken's side, as well as the pack he carried, were now both slick with mud from his fall. But after James asked if he needed help, Ken insisted he was fine. James kept an eye on him as they walked back to camp, and thankfully didn't see any limping or signs of pain. Only an embarrassed and slightly bruised ego.

'So we pack up and head straight out?' James asked as they walked.

'I guess so,' Ken replied. 'Though we're still going to need to camp again at least once. Don't forget, we've spent two nights here already, so even if we ran the whole way back, it'd still be well into tomorrow before we got out. Not that our energy levels would let us go on for that long without rest, of course.'

James knew that Ken made a valid point, and it was one he'd already considered. He checked his watch, seeing that it was already past noon. 'I agree,' he said. 'How about we get some food back at the camp before we set off? I'm feeling pretty weak already. Then, we discard what we can and make up as much ground as possible while we still have daylight to work with. We camp again come nightfall, and hope we get clear of the forest tomorrow. Then we can get back to Amaley and go to the police. They'll be much better equipped to find Tony out here.'

'And what if another one of us goes missing?' Roberta asked. Her voice sounded distant, almost like she was talking in her sleep.

'I don't know,' James admitted. It was something else he had been thinking about quite a lot, in truth. Given they had no idea what had happened to Tony, only relying on Roberta's story—that the creepy old woman pulled him from the tent in the night—there was every chance it could happen again. James felt that the odds of having an uneventful night were slim at best.

But what else could they do? Searching for Tony had yielded nothing, unless you counted Ken's discovery as some kind of result, which James didn't, and they couldn't keep looking forever. Blindly wandering the forest, getting more and more lost, would not lead to anything good. And they certainly couldn't just lie down and wait for help to arrive.

So they had to try and escape. Which meant Roberta had been right that morning.

'I think one of us should be awake at all times when we camp,' Ken said. 'We can take turns, do it in shifts. That way, if anything happens, the person standing guard can alert the others. At least that way we'll get a little rest.'

It was a shitty plan, but as fine a one as any James could see, given the circumstances. It still didn't make him feel any better, or any less on edge, but at least it was a course of action.

They eventually reached the campsite again, and it was a welcome sight to James. He had been half expecting to find that all of their tents had been destroyed during their absence, but everything seemed as it was before.

The group quickly stored their packs, and then Ken got to work with the stove, cooking a dehydrated meal of chicken and noodles. After they had eaten, the camp was disassembled in less than an hour, and then they packed up the essentials, leaving behind a lot of very expensive equipment.

It pained James to do it, knowing how much of their own money they had sunk into it all, but he knew deep down it was the right thing to do. Things had become much more serious since yesterday, feeling like life or death.

They made sure everything was cased up as best as possible and stashed the equipment in a large bush at the base of a tree, which would at least offer it some protection. Maybe, one day in the near future, someone could come back out and reclaim it.

For now, however, they kept their handheld cameras and Roberta's digital audio recorder, as they took up next-to-no space and were not heavy. If they had to explain a death after their escape, perhaps the footage would act as evidence of some kind.

With the campsite now behind them, the trio marched through the forest, following Ken's directions as he guided them forward. The smell of pine intensified and the skies began to darken above.

'Rain's coming,' Ken said. 'We may have to camp earlier than we thought.'

'Can't we just get wet?' James asked.

'We can, but putting up our tents in the rain will be difficult.'

Roberta was still quiet.

'Let's keep going for now,' James said, feeling the wind pick up. 'If we need to stop, then we can stop.'

Ken nodded, and they pushed on.

The wind got stronger and stronger and started whistling through the trees. The very air around them sounded angry and felt charged with energy. Whatever weather was coming, it was serious.

Fuck.

James knew the storm was going to delay things. He was about to suggest finding a good spot to camp when Ken cried out, pointing off into the trees to their left.

'Tony!'

20

KEN WAS off and running before he had time to process the whole thing, and calls from James to hold on and wait were ignored—barely even registering.

He had seen movement out the corner of his eye. And, after turning his head, he'd seen what he'd been hoping to since the previous night: there Tony was, standing off in the distance and waving—beckoning Ken to go to him. The image had taken a moment to sink in, and Tony had since stepped behind a tree, even before Ken had shouted his name out in shock.

He heard James call out again as he ran, and also heard both James and Roberta running after him. But surely, if they'd seen what he had, they would have been matching Ken's speed to get to their friend.

Because Tony was alive. And, in the brief moment Ken had seen him, he looked fine and well.

'Over here!' Ken yelled back. 'I saw him! I saw him!'

'Wait, God damn it!' James shouted back.

However, Ken was in no mood for arguments or dissent in the ranks. His friend was alive, and Ken intended to help him. He reached the tree Tony had moved behind, with the others catching up in short order.

But Tony was not there.

However, when Ken looked up, it turned out Tony was farther ahead, again waving.

'There,' Ken said, pointing.

'Jesus Christ,' James uttered in shock. Ken took off again, reassured that James had obviously seen him too. And yet, even in the face of that, James still shouted for Ken to stop. The weather continued to worsen, with the wind gaining strength, now sounding like a furious howl.

'Ken, what the fuck are you doing?' James shouted, running close behind. Ken felt James' hand grab at his back-pack, but he managed to shrug it off. 'Just look at him!' James screamed.

Ken was looking at him. He was looking at a friend who needed their help, and who was beckoning them to him. But again, Tony stepped away, moving out of view.

A pang of déjà vu sprang up in Ken as he remembered chasing down that walking corpse earlier when he had been led to the village.

But this was different, he convinced himself, as Tony was not some decaying wreck of a body. It was their colleague, just as Ken remembered him prior to him disappearing last night.

However, when Ken eventually reached the point he had last seen Tony—almost being blown from his feet by the battering wind as he did—he found that Tony was once again gone. And yet again, as before, Ken saw him up ahead. And so the sequence began once more, with James still yelling at him to stop.

But it seemed that Roberta was not on the same page as James.

'What's your problem?' she shouted at him.

'Can't either of you see it?' James replied as he ran, out of breath and panting hard.

Suddenly, Ken felt a great force hit him from behind, powerful enough to knock him over and drive him face first into the wet leaves and dirt. A heavy weight pressed into him, partially pinning him to the ground. Ken managed to wiggle over onto his back to see that James had tackled him and had now sat above him.

'Just stop,' James pleaded.

Ken fought against the younger man in a fit of anger, reaching a hand up to James' face to push him away. 'What is your problem?' Ken seethed.

'James!' Roberta shouted, pulling at him. 'Get off, what's gotten into you? We need to help Tony!'

'That isn't Tony!' James screamed. 'Why can't any of you see it?'

'See what?' Roberta asked as Ken managed to kick his way out from James' hold.

'It wasn't Tony!' James yelled. 'Didn't you see the state of him? There's no way that rotting mess could still be alive. It wasn't Tony!'

To say that those words threw Ken was an understatement. To him, Tony had seemed himself and looked no different. 'He was fine,' Ken stated.

James gave a confused look, then turned his head to Roberta, who nodded her confirmation. 'He looked okay to me,' she said.

'Well he didn't to me,' James answered, shaking his head. 'And doesn't that seem fucking odd? That we are seeing different things? If it really was Tony, then we would have all seen the same thing. And he wouldn't have been playing this fucking game, either, having us run after him only to disappear time and time again. Don't you get it? Something out here is toying with us. And if we follow it and go where it wants us to, then we are fucked.'

Ken's heart was beating rapidly in his chest, and he still felt the urge to run after Tony. The sight of him had been so real that Ken's instinct had been to run to his friend's aid.

Now, however, hearing what James had seen, and listening to what he was saying, it gave Ken reason to pause —his colleague was making sense. There was no reason for Tony to keep disappearing like that. And what the hell had James meant when he'd said, *did you see the state of him?*

Rain started to fall, light and fine droplets that threatened to intensify.

'Roberta?' Ken asked. 'Did he look fine to you?'

Roberta nodded. 'Yes. I didn't see anything wrong. And I think we should keep going. Tony is obviously out there, and he needs—'

'Ken,' James said, interrupting. 'Listen to reason. None of this makes any fucking sense. We are just going to get ourselves killed.' James then looked to Roberta. 'And why are you so eager to run off deeper into the forest all of a sudden? What's changed?'

Roberta snarled, then lashed out again—suddenly and viciously—slapping James once more across the face, letting out a growl like a wild animal as she did.

'Fuck you,' she spat. Ken saw James clench his jaw after the blow, and a furious expression spread over his face.

'No,' he replied through gritted teeth. 'Fuck you.'

He then stepped forward and pushed Roberta forcefully, hard enough that she toppled backwards and hit the ground. She looked up in shock.

'You pushed me!' Roberta exclaimed in disbelief.

'And you hit me,' James retorted.

Ken was taken aback by the sudden development, which now seemed to be swaying towards more serious violence as Roberta leapt back up to her feet and flung her hands out at James' face, claws bared. Ken, acting on impulse, managed to throw himself between the two and held Roberta back as she wriggled and fought against him. Thankfully, James did not try and retaliate. Ken seriously doubted he could keep them both away from each other at the same time. Though, from the scowl on James' face, it didn't seem like he was far from having to do so.

What the hell is happening to them?

Eventually, Ken managed to calm Roberta, and she stopped fighting to get to James—where Ken believed she would have clawed his eyes out, given the chance.

'Calm down, both of you!' Ken shouted, still standing between them. 'This is the last thing we need.'

Roberta slowly stopped fighting back, to Ken's eternal thanks, but the two settled into a stare-off. James, eventually, looked away and his cheeks flushed red with embarrassment.

'I'm sorry,' he said.

Roberta, however, gave no such ground. Her expression was like thunder, her gaze trained on James. Considering the two had tentatively discussed marriage only a few short months ago, it unnerved Ken to see how quickly they had turned on each other. And to also see the look of hate currently etched onto Roberta's face.

The rain continued to fall, now in heavy sheets, soaking them all and coming down faster and harder by the minute.

James backed up, putting distance between him and his girlfriend—if that's what she still was—and Ken could see the man looked ashamed with himself. 'I... I can't believe I did that,' he said softly, looking down to the ground. 'I don't know what came over me.' He then held up his head and looked straight at Roberta. 'I'm so sorry.'

It seemed a genuine apology.

Roberta wasn't having any of it, however. 'I don't care,' she replied. 'You can stick it up your arse.'

A terrible silence between them all ensued. Ken's urge to find Tony was still there, but things had settled, and now that the fog or irrationality had lifted, Ken could see the sense in what James had said.

If that had been Tony, then why hadn't he run over and joined them of his own accord? Why lead them off in this direction?

And the other troubling question Ken had was, why had Tony appeared different to James?

'We need to keep going,' Ken said.

'I don't think that's a good idea,' James replied, his voice still soft. 'I know it's hard to hear, Ken, but that wasn't Tony.'

'I'm starting to realise that,' Ken agreed. 'But that's not what I mean. We need to keep going to get back to the car. We need to get out of this forest.'

James looked surprised, but nodded in agreement.

'So are we just turning tail and leaving Tony?' Roberta asked.

As soon as she said it, Ken realised that James could well have been right about her. While pushing the woman over was unacceptable, her change in attitude was startling. Why was she now so keen to stay in this forest, especially longer than needed? Only hours earlier she had been pushing both Ken and James to do the sensible thing and run, despite not knowing where Tony was. In fact, Roberta had been adamant that he had been abducted by this Mother Sibbett figure, swearing she had seen the old woman take him.

But suddenly, that threat now seemed inconsequential to Roberta—or at least, less immediate.

'We don't have a choice,' Ken said. 'I don't know what it was we were chasing, but it obviously wasn't Tony. If it was, he would have called to us. He would have come to us, like James said, not lead us farther into the woods.'

'Sounds to me like you are both cowards,' Roberta replied defiantly. Her top lip was curled in a snarl, but Ken also noticed that she looked even more pale and gaunt than he remembered. Heavy purple bags hung beneath her eyes, and the skin of her cheeks had sunken. Roberta almost looked emaciated.

'Let's go,' Ken said simply, not in the mood for a debate. His heart was heavy at the thought of leaving his friend, but Ken suspected now that it would be pointless trying to find him. He'd followed a ghost before, and it had led Ken to its own hanging body. Ken had a terrible feeling that following Tony would yield a similar result.

He and James set off again back in the direction they had originally been heading. Ken hoped Roberta would follow. Thankfully, she did.

They walked for hours until the weather eventually eased up and night closed in. Ken held out as long as he could, but eventually knew they would have to camp. It was not something he was looking forward to, and he was concerned about what the night would bring.

BOTH TENTS WERE UP—THE three of them having decided they could not all squash into one—and they ate again. However, Roberta had no appetite. Instead of eating her portion, she stealthily tipped it down by the side of her tent.

And the single mouthful she had managed to eat only served to make her feel nauseous.

While food certainly did not appeal, the thought of the two men she was travelling with truly made her feel sick.

They were cowards.

Pathetic worms who had decided to turn tail and flee, leaving one of their group behind. Roberta was well aware that she had been of a similar mindset only hours ago... but now she knew better.

Her mind was gaining clarity. There was no need to run. In fact, she knew she needed to make sure they all stayed here. At least until they found Tony, she told herself.

It was the right thing to do. Yes. The right thing.

They would all stay here.

And perhaps meet Mother Sibbett. And see the village. And the Church of Holy Sin.

They may even be fortunate enough to indulge in the Ritual of Atonement—with Mother's blessing, of course.

Roberta looked to James.

He would make a good sacrifice. And she would make sure that the weasel would come to see the truth. And he would feel what Mother had to give him, too.

She would make him suffer as she was welcomed into the undead family of the Black Forest. She could feel Mother's approval in her mind as the thoughts danced through her consciousness... and Roberta didn't even realise she was smiling.

21

WHEN JAMES WAS AWAKENED from his sleep, he wasn't exactly sure of the hour. Initially startled, he felt something tickling his cheek, and something cold and wet pressing against his skin.

It was then that the smell around him triggered a realisation in his mind, and he turned to see Roberta leaning over him. She still looked different—almost ill—but there was a hungry glint in her eye. She bent down towards him, her hair brushing his face and tickling him again, and she pressed her cold, wet lips to his.

James couldn't see much in the dark, but he could see enough to know Roberta had slipped from most of her clothes, now wearing only underwear and a vest-top.

'Are you okay?' he asked.

She nodded and smiled. 'Fine,' she said and kissed him again, this time more passionately. Her tongue made its way into his mouth, and he instinctively began to kiss her back.

The taste was odd to James, but then neither of their personal hygiene was at its best. Regardless, he felt a tightening in his trousers as Roberta ran her hands through his hair, grabbing it roughly just as he liked it. James gently pulled his head away.

'You must be freezing,' he said.

'I'm okay,' she replied. He knew that wasn't true, as her body felt like a block of ice on top of him. He pulled open his sleeping bag. 'Here,' he said. 'Get in with me.'

She giggled, but did as instructed, pressing her body against his, thrusting her groin against his hard cock. Her mouth found his again, and she bit his lip.

'It'll get pretty hot in here soon,' she whispered seductively, then pulled at his trousers. 'You may want to take these off.'

This time he did as ordered, and they started to kiss again. He then ripped off her top, exposing her breasts, and began to bite at them, sucking at her erect nipples. Roberta flung her head back and pulled his face into her bosom firmly, moaning in the process.

James was soon inside of her, thrusting deep and shuddering with pleasure at the warm embrace around his dick. He pinned Roberta's hands to the tent floor and thrust down on her again as she squirmed and let out a gasp.

'Harder,' she whispered. He complied, thrusting deep, and she cried out, snaking her wrists free and clamping her hands to his back, pulling him farther into her.

'Harder!' she commanded again.

Somewhere, behind all of this animalistic lust, James was confused at yet another change in demeanour from Roberta. But, given how they had acted with each other only a few hours earlier, he was not about to give it too much thought. Things were far too intense for that right now, and far too pleasurable.

A tingling sensation at the head of his penis started to build as he pumped faster and faster; the feeling of Roberta's lithe body squirming and writhing beneath him was pushing him towards the edge. She continued to let out more moans of pleasure and her pelvic muscles tensed and clamped down on him.

James was very aware that the noise they were making could wake Ken, or even draw the attention of anyone—or anything—else in the vicinity. But right now, he just didn't fucking care. All he wanted was completion.

So he sped up his thrusting, feeling his climax getting closer and closer. But Roberta stopped, suddenly pushing him off.

'Not yet,' she whispered.

For a moment James was crestfallen, thinking she had used this as a way to get back at him for what he'd done earlier—getting him right to the height of excitement, only to deny him completely.

But it appeared Roberta just wanted things to go on a little longer. She rolled James to his back and mounted him, bearing down and letting his dick slide into her. Her writhing atop him quickly brought James back to the brink of orgasm once again. However, Roberta controlled things now, rocking and bucking as she wanted, but easing off when his squirming intensified too much. She pulled at his hair and leaned in, kissing him once more.

Again, there was an odd, unpleasant taste to the kiss. Metallic, somehow, though neither of them was bleeding as far as James could tell. Unless, he thought, she had cut his lip when biting him earlier. The idea of that just turned him on more, and Roberta then thrust a finger into his mouth for him to suck on.

Her rhythmic movements atop him were getting to be too much, but it turned out she was still not done. Roberta retrieved her discarded vest-top from the floor and stretched out the white material, lowering it to his head.

'This will be fun,' she said.

At first, he was hesitant and shook his head, but a quick flex of her pelvic muscles again brought about compliance from him, and James then let her wrap the fabric around his head and over his eyes. She pulled it tight and fastened the blindfold securely.

'Can you see?' she asked.

He shook his head. 'Not a thing.' It was the truth.

'Good,' she replied, and again began to expertly work his erect penis with her hips, building him to yet another orgasm. When he was close, Roberta climbed from him, again denying him.

'Noooo,' James groaned as his body was on the cusp of spasming. 'Don't stop, please.'

'All in good time, boy,' she replied.

Boy?

Never in all their years together had Roberta ever referred to him as *boy*. The thought quickly fell from James' mind, however, as he felt her hand grasp his erect cock, then he felt her hot breath on the head.

She let out a long 'Mmmmmmmm,' sound, and put him in her wet mouth, clamping her lips tightly around him. James' body locked as her teeth then pressed down, sharply, drawing a gasp from him. For a moment he thought she would bring her teeth together completely, shearing off his penis, but instead she took the rest of him, gulping him down into her throat. She then slowly drew her head back, sucking and slurping as she went, before diving back down. She repeated this several more times before coming almost all the way off, running her tongue over his sensitive head. James was squirming wildly beneath her, struggling to hold on as she played with him, getting him close to release, but then pulling her head away, allowing him an agonising moment to calm down.

James didn't know how much more of this denial he could take.

'Open your mouth,' she said. He did, expecting her to again insert a digit. However, he felt the ticking of her hair on his face. Thinking her lips would find his, James was shocked at what came next.

He heard a spitting sound and then felt a glob of thick, foul-tasting liquid hit his tongue. He instantly gagged.

'What the fuck!' he yelled out, disgusted. James then went to spit it back out, but her hand clamped over his mouth.

'Swallow,' she ordered.

He was about to rip the blindfold off and yell at her for what she'd done—after all, he liked a little kink, but that little act had done nothing for him—when she again took hold of his penis with her full lips. Still keeping a hand over his mouth, she began to suck.

Feelings of repulsion were quickly forgotten—popping up briefly as he involuntarily swallowed the vile substance —and Roberta then got back on top of him.

There was no playful denial this time. Though James couldn't see her very well, he felt every movement as the gyrating on his penis became full-on bouncing, with him thrusting his hips up into her in time with Roberta's movements.

He could hold on no longer. James' body locked and he came, spilling an orgasm up inside of her, crying out in pleasure as he did.

Roberta, too, wailed as her muscles spasmed and clamped over him, with her orgasm more prolonged. He heard her short, sharp breaths as his orgasm peaked and dropped.

After a moment of neither one moving, simply enjoying the spent feeling, James slowly removed the makeshift blindfold. He planned to bring Roberta down into his arms and cuddle her. After all, this had been unexpected, but perhaps just what they both needed. He would even thank her for it.

However, when his eyes focused on her, he did not see a look of happiness on Roberta's face in the dark. While she looked flushed, her expression was not a friendly one. Roberta quickly rolled off of him and began to put her clothes back on.

'Are you okay?' he asked her, confused again.

She ignored him and finished wrapping herself up before getting back into her sleeping bag and facing away from him.

'Roberta?' he asked.

'Fuck you,' she said. 'I'm going to sleep.'

James was staggered. *What the fuck was wrong with her?*

'Are you serious?' he asked, incredulous.

'Yup,' she replied. 'I got mine. Now fuck off and leave me alone.'

James could not figure out what the hell had just happened between them. Roberta had initiated the whole thing and had then given him one of the best orgasms he'd ever had—minus the spitting, of course. And now, she was back to hating him, it seemed.

Feeling drained, James was too tired to argue further. He was indeed mad, and wanted to yell—to tell Roberta to go fuck herself. But in the end, he pushed his anger down and rolled over as well.

Neither said another word, and soon James dropped off into a deep, exhausted sleep.

ROBERTA SOON HEARD JAMES' light snores next to her. Part of her wanted to put her hands around his neck and not stop squeezing until he turned purple. The satisfaction he'd just given her had been meagre, and she wanted more.

She craved it.

So, swallowing the build-up of black liquid that had accumulated in her mouth, she slithered a hand down into her underwear.

Careful not to wake anyone, Roberta was still rough and fierce as she masturbated, her nails digging into the sensitive nub of her sex. She knew she was drawing blood—could feel it on her fingers—and this drove her over the edge once more.

22

KEN WAS UP EARLY, as soon as the morning light broke. He'd had another unsettling dream after falling asleep—which wasn't easy after hearing James and Roberta release their frustrations. But, as unpleasant as it had been to hear, hopefully it would help repair some bridges between the two of them.

And, thankfully, no one else had been taken in the night. James had emerged from his tent not long after Ken and informed him that Roberta was still sleeping. The two of them stood together, eyes scouring the campsite for signs of trespassing or disturbance. It was a relief to Ken that they found nothing.

'Things better between you now?' Ken asked.

James shrugged. 'Should they be?'

'Well, it sounded like you made up last night.'

James' face, paler than normal, now flushed red. 'Yeah... sorry about that. Though I still don't think things are right between us. She was pretty off with me after we'd finished.'

'Oh,' Ken said, not knowing how else to respond. He tried to lighten the mood. 'So, she got hers, then?'

James chuckled. 'She said the exact same thing.' He then poked the toe of his boot into the grass, pulling up clumps of mud. 'How are you doing?' he asked Ken.

'I'm not sure. I'm scared, if I'm being honest. I never thought anything like this would happen.'

'I hear you,' James replied. 'I can't tell you how excited I was at first when we heard those voices. And then what we saw on camera. I thought we had it. Definitive proof. I thought we were going to be superstars. But now, with Tony missing...'

James didn't finish his sentence, but he didn't have to. 'I know what you mean,' Ken said. 'I just wish I knew what happened to him. I can't understand it.'

'Do you believe what Roberta said? About her seeing him get taken in the night?'

Ken sighed and shrugged. 'I honestly don't know. I have no reason *not* to believe her, given what we've all experienced. But this is all hard for me to get my head around.'

James nodded. 'Agreed. But you think that Tony could still be alive?'

Ken didn't answer, because he didn't know how to. Instead, he let the silence hang. Ken wanted Tony to still be alive, to be out there, somewhere, waiting for them to find him. That's what his heart told him. But his head—cold and logical—told a different story. It told him that it was too late for his friend, and if they didn't get out of the Black Forest soon, they would all meet a similar fate.

'We should get moving,' Ken said, shifting the topic of conversation. 'Get some breakfast to give us energy, then go.'

'Are you still okay with that?' James asked. 'The plan of getting out of here, I mean. Even without...'

Yet again, James trailed off, not needing to finish.

Ken nodded. 'It's the right thing to do. Might not feel like it, but it is, I guess.'

'Okay. I'll go wake Roberta.'

James patted Ken on the shoulder as he passed, leaving Ken to get to work pulling together a quick and basic breakfast for them all.

Roberta soon emerged from her tent with James, looking even worse than she had the previous day. Her skin had paled further, and she'd lost just about all of her healthy Mediterranean complexion. Amazingly, she seemed to be even more gaunt as well and looked positively anorexic. Ken had to stop from letting his mouth hang open in shock at her appearance. Could someone really lose that much weight in such a short span of time without being ill?

And that, of course, raised more questions. What if she *was* ill? And, if so, what kind of illness could have done something so drastic to her in just a few days?

On top of that, her eyes looked heavy, with dark rings circling the undersides. The whites were severely bloodshot and her hair looked thin and greasy, making her scalp visible beneath.

Ken made a note to speak to James about it in private. If they did make it out of the forest alive, then Roberta needed to see a doctor urgently.

With breakfast finished and the tents packed away, Ken consulted his compass and notes to check on progress. He was confident they were heading in the right direction, roughly, though nothing really looked familiar from their journey in. There was every chance, however, that they were coming out along a slightly different line, but still in the same general direction, so he wasn't too concerned. As long as they got clear of the forest, finding the car from there would be a simple task of skirting the edge until they came across it.

It was a little before nine in the morning when they set off again, this time walking side by side where space allowed, the previous single-file formation abandoned. The weather was cold now, colder than it had been the rest of the week. And no more than an hour into their trek, another bout of rain began. It started light, but within the space of twenty minutes came crashing down. The wind again picked up as well, just as it had the day before, and it whipped around them, harshly blowing the driving rain into their faces.

If this wasn't a full storm, then Ken thought it surely wasn't far off from being one.

Progress slowed as the three of them had to constantly shield their eyes from the torrential onslaught as it drove into their faces.

It almost seemed to Ken like something was trying to hinder their escape. And, if that was true, and whatever entity resided here could dictate the very weather... well, that made him feel truly insignificant.

Like they could all be picked off at will. Just as Tony had been.

Come midday, they had not made anywhere near the progress Ken had hoped for, having been slowed considerably by the adverse conditions. The ground had practically become a bog they needed to wade through, and on more than one occasion one of them had lost their footing. By the time they stopped for a break, hiding beneath the canopy of a tree, they were all filthy—coated in mud and drenched to the core. Their waterproof clothing wasn't able to withstand the constant and heavy sheets of rain, with the branches above not affording much protection at all.

'How much longer do you think this will keep up?' James asked, shouting over the howling wind.

'I have no idea,' Ken yelled back. The storm, such as it was, showed no signs of diminishing. The sky above, covered with black clouds, was as dark as a late dusk.

They were all breathing heavily, showing signs of the exertions they had been making over the last three hours. But they had yielded minimal results. Ken knew that even if they could pick up the pace for the remainder of the day, it was unlikely they would get clear of the forest—not before morning, at least.

Which meant they would have to spend another night here. And while last night had passed without incident, Ken had a horrible feeling they would not be as lucky a second time. Ken let himself drop back against the trunk of the tree they were under and tried to get his breathing under control. He pondered what they should do: get some more food in their stomachs to give them a little more energy, or just push on?

Progress would still be slow, but it would be preferable to not moving at all. However, realistically, how much longer could they keep going like this?

He looked off through the pouring rain. It might take everything they had in their tank, but he knew they needed to get out of here today—camping again could not be an option.

Whatever it took, even if they had to push themselves to the point of failure, it had to be done.

As he continued looking out into the trees, Ken's breath suddenly caught in his throat.

After seeing the first one, he looked around to see another. And another. *How had he missed something so obvious.*

There were scores of them standing out there in the pouring rain, stock-still, between trees that now appeared to have blackened.

Their ruined clothing looked hundreds of years old, given the basic styling, and their mangled and rotting bodies showed they were not among the living.

However, they were not like the corpse guide Ken had seen yesterday, either. These things were different.

Their faces... oh God, their faces: twisted and inhuman.

'Jesus Christ!' James cried out in utter terror, finally seeing the same thing. There was no way all three of them could have missed these horrors until now, which suggested to Ken that silent watchers had only just made themselves known.

He quickly turned to run, but his right leg did not move as intended, and he instead fell to the wet earth, sinking into it. He turned in the mud as rain splashed all around him and saw that something was holding on to him, protruding from the ground and grasping onto his ankle.

An arm had snaked up from the mud, adorned in tattered and decomposing flesh. The fingers of its hand gripped tighter.

Ken screamed.

23

Upon seeing the monstrosities spread out in the trees ahead of them, James instinctively grabbed Roberta's arm and ran, dragging her along behind him. It was the opposite direction from the one they needed to go to escape, but that mattered little, given what they faced.

The only thing that stopped him in his tracks was the yell from Ken.

'Help!'

James turned to see Ken on the ground, struggling with something on his leg. It took James a moment to realise what was emerging from the mud, and he could scarcely believe it.

An arm had taken hold of Ken, who struggled against it. The body that was attached to the appendage then pulled itself from the mud, rising up into a sitting position; it was little more than a skeleton, with sparse chunks of mottled flesh clinging to the bones.

'Help!' Ken screamed again, wrestling with the impossible thing.

James froze for a moment, debating turning tail and

fleeing with Roberta. The impulse was strong, but he managed to overcome his survival instinct and sprint back to Ken. It was a short distance to cover, and those things out in the trees did not appear to be moving any closer.

And James was also well aware that Ken was useful to him, being the best prepared among them to survive out in the wilderness. A sharp contrast to what James had previously thought about their leader. Now he was the one James felt they needed most to survive.

And perhaps that thought was what caused him to act so quickly: not out of concern or some altruistic drive, just simple necessity.

James quickly reached Ken and grabbed the man's flailing arm, yanking him with as much strength as he could gather. Thankfully, it was enough, with the muddy ground giving little resistance. This allowed James to pull Ken free of the grasp of the skeletal thing. Ken slipped through the mud and kicked away the reaching hands.

When James pulled Ken completely free and up to his feet, they both ran, quickly reaching Roberta and then heading farther into the trees, away from the mass of bodies that had barricaded their way out.

The rain still pelted down at a ferocious rate and the wind battered the group as they ran, blindly, without paying any real attention to the direction they moved. They just concentrated on getting away from the horrors behind them, ducking and weaving through the trees, hoping to put as much distance as they could between themselves and the demons they had just seen.

James' lungs soon began to burn in protest and a fiery stitch developed in his side. He heaved and panted, but still forced his body to move as quickly as it could, powering through the mud. Eventually, however, his untrained body could take no more, and he had to stop before he fell.

'I can't...' he wheezed out, unable to finish. Ken and Roberta halted their progress and turned around. They both looked exhausted as well, and concern for James forced them to stop.

Ken jogged back to him and tried to pull James on. 'We need to keep going,' he urged.

James tried, pushing himself off again, but managed less than a hundred paces before he fell to the ground. James knew he wasn't the fittest person in the world, but ever since he'd awakened that morning, he had felt much weaker than usual. Something was wrong.

'I can't,' he repeated between breaths. 'I need to stop.'

James then looked back, letting his eyes scour the direction they had all come from, but he saw nothing following them. He also noted that the rain and wind had eased up.

'Okay,' Ken said, finally. 'But we can't stop for long. Those things could be close behind.'

James nodded, all too aware of that fact, and he gulped down large swathes of air in an attempt to sooth his burning lungs.

Roberta stood silently nearby, just staring at James. But her eyes were vacant, as if she were looking right through him. James wasn't even sure that she was registering the danger they were in, danger that felt very real and urgent. Things had been bad before, of course, with Tony going missing. Although, there was always the chance, however slight, that something explainable had happened to him— that they weren't up against and hunted by some unexplainable force.

But that uncertainty was gone now. And worse, whatever evil was behind all of this, it didn't look like it wanted to let them leave the forest and had blocked their escape. Before he could stop it, an uncontrollable panic rose up from James' gut and settled in his chest and caused it to tighten, making his breathing difficult.

James had never been one to suffer from panic attacks, but that changed in an instant, and he started to hyper-ventilate.

'Keep calm,' Ken told him, without sounding it himself. He squatted down next to James. 'Breathe deeply.'

James tried, but it seemed beyond him to halt the feeling of utter helplessness that was overwhelming him. 'We're going to die here, aren't we,' James stated.

'No,' Ken stated. 'No, we aren't. But we need to keep our heads.'

James buried his face in his hands and started to sob, unable to stop himself—the weight of the situation taking hold. At that moment, he felt like even trying to save them-selves was an exercise in futility.

He then heard Roberta chuckle.

'So weak,' she said in a soft yet condescending voice. 'Weak little man.'

A flash of anger pierced James' feeling of helplessness. He still couldn't understand why his girlfriend was being like this, getting more and more uncaring and cruel. And now, after seeing him in such a desperate way, she had decided to mock him.

'What the fuck is wrong with you?' he snapped, jumping up to his feet. 'Seriously, what has got into your fucking head?'

'Don't shout at me!' Roberta screamed back, the vacant look on her face replaced by a sudden rage. 'I'll claw your fucking eyes out.'

'Roberta, James,' Ken said, holding up his hands. 'Stop it, both of you. Please.'

'Fuck you,' Roberta said. 'Fuck you both. Acting like you know what's going on. Always thinking you're in control. Well, you're not now, are you? You're lost and scared. Scared little boys.'

'No, Roberta,' James said. 'We're lost. We're *all* lost, and we're all in danger. That includes you.'

Roberta just shrugged. 'Then why am I not worried?'

'Honestly?' James asked. 'Because I think you're losing it. Your mind has snapped, and you're going fucking crazy. You're not worried because you no longer understand the situation.'

She then laughed again. 'Oh, I understand things just fine, James. Much more than you do. But, for what it's worth, you are right about one thing. You *are* going to die. And soon.'

'Fuck you!' James replied and took a step towards her, the rage that coursed through his body now rising in intensity. He felt Ken's meaty palm on his chest, stopping him from going any farther forward.

'Leave it,' Ken said. 'We don't need this right now.'

James looked at the older man, knowing that he was probably right. It didn't sit well with James, however, and as he turned back to Roberta, he saw her smile at him like a spoiled child, giving him a wave in the process. She was clearly taunting him, actually wanting him to react.

And boy, did he want to react.

But he didn't. He managed to swallow down his anger again, like he had the previous night, and tried to ignore her, turning instead back to Ken. 'Okay, I'll leave it. But what do we do now?'

However, Ken wasn't looking at James, but behind him,

off into the distance. And the older man's face had drained of blood.

'We run,' Ken said. James turned as well, gasping in horror upon seeing those things again. They had returned —the entities from before—and once again waited among the trees, less than a hundred metres away from the group. They watched on with hungry, yellow eyes, and their faces had twisted into something... unexplainable.

Something inhuman.

James didn't need to be told again, and he followed Ken's lead, forcing himself to move. This time, however, he did not grab Roberta's arm to pull her with them. She did follow on her own, though, and kept pace.

A pang of guilt swelled through James as he realised he'd let her behaviour affect him so much that he was actually willing to leave her behind. Regardless of how fucking strangely she was acting, had things really come to that?

The thought was quickly pushed from his mind as the need to survive took over instead. He followed Ken, who was up ahead, and the man suddenly bore right with a shriek. James was confused at first, but then he saw one of those things ahead, unnaturally tall, with half of its gangly, naked body exposed from behind a black tree. James followed Ken, avoiding the monstrosity in front of him.

Every time he cast a glance back over his shoulder, James saw those things. Though they always appeared stock-still, they were always there, somehow keeping pace with the progress the group was making, appearing whenever James' eyes turned to look back.

'We need to move quicker!' James shouted with what little breath he had in his lungs. The stitch had returned, but he didn't have the luxury to stop.

They sprinted for what seemed like an eternity through

the forest as the rain and wind died down to nothing. James let himself look back again and saw that they were finally gone, no longer in pursuit.

'Wait,' he heard Ken call out, but it was too late. By the time James had turned to look back ahead, he had already passed Ken, and hadn't seen the reason both he and Roberta had stopped.

James felt his legs kick out at open air for a moment before he fell down a sharp slope, one he hadn't even known was there. Head over heels he tumbled, rolling down the slick, muddy surface of the steep hill. He eventually skidded to a stop on his back two-thirds of the way down, his body ravaged with pain, having hit loose branches and rocks on the way down.

He let out a groan and opened his eyes, panic still coursing through him. As James looked out ahead, his body froze.

Ancient, dilapidated wooden houses sat between the trees before him, clustered around fairly open ground where the trees were much less dense. Behind the circle of houses stood a stone structure, one that resembled a simple church.

James instantly knew what this was—the very same thing Ken had found earlier, only in an entirely different place.

It was the lost village.

24

KEN WAS quick to make his way down towards James, who had now reached the bottom of the slope. Roberta followed behind carefully—uneasy on her feet as she, too, made the descent. When they all gathered at the base, Ken stepped forward, scarcely believing what lay before them.

It was the same cluster of buildings he had seen yesterday, of that he had no doubt. There were basic houses consisting of timber walls and doors—although many had fallen from their hinges—and pitched roofs constructed from rudimentary tiles or thatched straw. The windows to the houses were small, single-pane affairs with rotted wooden frames.

These dwellings were, as before, nestled between the trees, the trunks of which were again black, matching the wood of the houses as well.

The buildings circled an open space that was almost devoid of trees, and it seemed to serve as a village centre with a stone well at the middle. Behind this open area, but directly in Ken's line of sight, was the building that stood out most: a small stone church. Simple in its design and form, the church was made from random grey blocks and had a pitched tile roof. The front of the building, which was one of the gable ends, contained a large and strong-looking wooden entrance door. Above the door sat a high, thin window that had been boarded up, and at the head of the wall an iron crucifix rose up from the pointed apex. On this cross a body—old and decayed—was mounted, arms out to its side and head lolled down to its chest.

Given that all of the windows he could see had been boarded up, and the fact that the slate roof sagged and was covered with moss, Ken got the impression that the church had long since been abandoned. The rest of the village, too. At least, that's what he hoped.

Regardless, this was without a doubt the same village Ken had found yesterday, but somehow it had shifted location, because it was clear to him that they had not run far enough back into the forest to get to the same place he had previously seen it. Not even close. Hell, they should have been about a day's walk away from that spot. And the layout of the village, while roughly the same, had adjusted enough to suit its surroundings.

The trees here were much less dense, allowing the buildings to sit closer together, and the centre of the village was almost entirely unobstructed, whereas previously the dwellings just seemed to be tucked between the trees wherever possible. At the time, Ken had assumed that the forest had grown around those buildings over the years, but then the village had vanished, and now this one was here for them to see.

'I don't believe it,' James uttered. He looked back up the incline behind them, wide-eyed, and Ken gazed up, too. He knew what James was thinking. Those things could still be coming. However, the crest of the bank was clear.

A realisation then struck, one that should have come to him straight away. While the mass of bodies had indeed blocked their exit from the forest, he understood they served a different purpose after appearing both behind and, when needed, in front of them, serving to push the three of them in a specific direction.

Right to this spot.

'We need to keep going,' James said. 'Those things—'

'They aren't following us anymore,' Ken stated.

James turned to look at him, his brow furrowed in confusion. 'What do you mean?'

'They weren't chasing us, James. They were *guiding* us. Shepherding us to this place.' He held out his hands, gesturing to the village before them.

Ken saw the realisation draw over James' face. 'Fuck,' he said. 'Then surely we need to get away from here. Nothing good can be waiting for us.'

'And how do we do that?' Ken asked. 'If we flee, don't you think those things will just push us right back here? We wouldn't get anywhere. Unless you think we have a chance by running right through them?'

After a moment's consideration, James shook his head. His body slumped, defeated. 'Then what do we do?' he asked.

Roberta started to walk away from them slowly, towards the buildings ahead. 'We look around,' she said, her voice almost happy. She then stopped and turned to them with an odd smile. 'Let's see who's home.'

'Roberta, wait!' Ken snapped, but she merely giggled and took off jogging, well out of his reach.

'She's going to get us killed,' Ken said to James.

James gave a nod. 'I agree,' he said. 'And part of me thinks she wants to.'

Ken didn't want to believe that.

Regardless of how unhinged Roberta seemed to be acting, and despite the stress she was clearly under, Ken didn't think she was the type of person to purposely cause any of them any harm. And Ken wasn't the type of person to simply stand by and let harm come to any of his group, either.

'Come on,' Ken said, pulling James along with him. 'We need to get her under control.'

James let out a spiteful snort, but he followed along. 'Good luck with that.'

Roberta skipped ahead along a muddy pathway leading to the village's centre, and peered into the well, which was made up of a circular, crumbling wall of stone that matched that of the church.

'Ohhhhh,' she said, obviously seeing something within, and giggled again.

Ken and James followed slowly, keeping their eyes on the surrounding buildings. Ken could detect no movement from within any of them, but still felt exposed as they walked into the middle of the village. They then reached the smiling Roberta, and Ken asked, 'What is it?'

'Look,' she said, pointing down inside.

Ken and James shared a glance before circling to the other side of the well, putting the circumference of it between them and Roberta. It was an instinctive move on Ken's part, as he had a horrible feeling Roberta would attempt to push him inside should he lean over and peer in.

So much for thinking she would never do them harm.

Clearly, he was just as wary of her and her mental state as James was. Once away from her reach, they both looked inside, and Ken gasped, his heart in his mouth at the awful sight below him.

Bodies.

Heaped on top of one another, and all completely naked. The skin on these corpses was the mottled white and purple of the long since deceased. However, these bodies had not decomposed over time, like the thing Ken had seen yesterday, or like the entities that had barred their escape earlier. Arms and legs intertwined with torsos and heads as the cadavers were mashed tightly together, packing the inside of the well. Men and women filled this mass grave, but that was not all.

Some bodies were smaller.

A foul stench immediately rose from the gaping hole of death beneath them and assaulted their senses. Ken gagged and backpedaled as James turned and vomited, a string of yellowy bile hanging from his mouth.

Ken was close to doing the same, but held the fabric of his sleeve over his nose and took steady, calming breaths through his mouth.

Real or not, that was the most horrific thing Ken had ever seen. Especially considering the age of some of the victims down there, which brought back memories of his own—

'Over there,' James said, interrupting Ken's line of thought. Though still doubled over, with his face red and eyes watering, James was pointing. Ken followed the gesture to the old church behind them and saw what James was pointing at.

The large door was slowly gliding open, swinging inwards into the darkness with a gentle creak.

No one emerged from the church, giving no indication as to who had opened the door, but Ken knew they were being beckoned inside.

'I think we should go in,' Roberta said, clearly excited.

'Not a fucking chance,' James replied, coughing again, and spitting globs of something black to the ground.

James had put plenty of distance between himself and that pile of bodies within that well, but the smell that wafted out was overpowering, and he was struggling to get his gagging under control. Ken continued to move farther away from it as well, unable to stand that horrific stench. Roberta, however, seemed completely unfazed.

'Oh, James, where's your sense of adventure?' Roberta asked, teasingly. 'You two still have your cameras, don't you? So why not go and get some more evidence? That's why we came here, after all. You should be recording this. All of it. We've found the legendary village, said to have vanished. Isn't it amazing? And now we are being called. There are answers waiting for us inside that church, James, I just know it. Don't you want to see what this place wants to show us?'

Again, James shook his head. 'No, we don't need to know. We need to leave.'

Ken agreed completely, of course he did, but he still didn't think they would get very far. Whatever it was in the forest that was stalking them... it wanted them here. It wouldn't let them go.

Then Ken heard something that made his heart freeze. It was the cry of someone young, coming from within the church, echoing out from it. The thing that chilled him most, however, was that he recognised the feminine voice as it shouted out a single, pained word.

'*Daddy.*'

25

JAMES HEARD the haunting cry from the church as well. It was the sound of a young girl in distress.

It caused the hairs on his arms to rise, certainly, but when he looked over to Ken, James saw that the sound was having a far more profound effect on the older man.

Ken looked ashen and close to tears.

Of all the fucked-up things they had seen and heard so far—top of that list being the sickening mass grave behind them—that call, while unsettling, was not something James reacted strongly to.

So why was Ken so evidently distressed by it? The answer came in a single word from Ken.

'Amy...'

James had no idea who Amy was to Ken, but jumped into action when Ken started running towards the stone church. He grabbed hold of Ken's arm and managed to spin him around.

'What the hell are you doing?' he asked. 'You can't go in there.'

'I have to,' Ken said as tears started to fall down his cheeks, streaking the dirt that coated them. 'Amy is in there.'

Ken tried to turn away again, but James stopped him. 'Who the hell is Amy? What's going on?'

Ken didn't take his eyes off the building, and they both heard the call again.

'*Daddy.*'

Ken started to sob. 'That's... that's my daughter.'

The revelation caught James off guard, as he hadn't been aware that Ken even had a daughter. James was so startled that Ken was able to shrug off his grip and again sprint towards the church, this time unhindered. But James knew there was no way Ken's daughter was really inside that place. It was a trick, played by whatever malevolent force had been toying with them all along. Why couldn't Ken see that?

Roberta giggled like a child herself, enjoying what was unfolding. He turned to her and scowled, but she just twirled a lock of thin, greasy hair around her finger and laughed again. 'He's going to die in there, you know,' she said.

James tensed his fists, so dearly wanting to swing at her. But instead, given that she could well be right, he sprinted after Ken. Considering the age difference between the two, James would have hoped he could have easily made up the distance, but the strength it took for him to run, even over this small distance, quickly sapped his energy. He immediately felt weak and drained again, and dizzy too.

Considering all they had been through recently, both mentally and physically, there was a good chance James was coming down with an illness—which he could scarcely afford right now. Perhaps that would explain it? He coughed and spat as he ran, the streak of liquid dripping from his mouth disconcertingly dark. And no matter how hard he tried, James could not seem to gain any ground on Ken, who disappeared inside of the church and into the darkness beyond.

James thought about stopping—considered it strongly— not wanting to know what was waiting inside that place. But he wasn't too far behind and felt he had a good chance of pulling Ken out of there. Also, whereas before he'd aided Ken because the man was a necessity to his own survival, now he just felt the need to help a friend. If Ken had truly heard the voice of his daughter, James could not imagine how confusing that must have been.

But he needed to get Ken to see things clearly and realise his daughter was not here; she would likely be wher- ever she had been before, hopefully safe and sound somewhere.

So he gritted his teeth and carried on, following Ken inside. As he crossed the threshold, James felt a noticeable, oppressive feeling fall over him, as if the darkness itself actually had weight to it. The air was also thick with a musty, potent smell.

James' eyes soon adjusted to the sudden absence of natural daylight, cut off thanks to the boarded windows, and saw that the church was lit by flickering candles, giving off an eerie glow.

James looked down the rest of the building's interior, but wished he hadn't.

The layout was what he would have imagined from a small, simple church such as this, with rows of wooden pews on either side of a central aisle. At the front, towards the other end, was a raised section that contained a pulpit and altar.

James wasn't a particularly religious person, but what he

saw down there he immediately understood to be an insult against God.

Bodies in various stages of decay had been strewn about —some whole, many not. The surroundings also had a dark-red palette to them, thanks to the gallons of spilt blood that wetted the floor and splattered the walls. Organs and intestines were strung up like decorations, looping over rafters and twirling around rudimentary effigies of Christ, wrapping around his neck and draping over his shoulders like a shroud.

And, while some of the corpses looked to have been merely dumped or discarded randomly, many had been positioned quite deliberately, their bodies propped and shaped, tied to sticks of wood with twine in order to hold their pose. Some had even been stitched together in sickening violent and sexual acts.

Two of them had their mouths sewn together—hands restrained behind their backs—as they were being sodomised by other macabre marionettes. The hands of the assailants grasped around the bound victims' necks. Another lay prone on the ground with its stomach open. A group kneeled close, heads lowered into the opening, like pigs feeding at a trough. There were even unfortunate corpses stuck and intertwined with beasts of the field.

Beyond all of this, situated on the raised area to the front, sat another body, this one markedly different than the others. With the wooden pulpit off to the left-hand side, and a simple altar behind it, the figure sat central to the width of the room, heels pulled into its crotch in a cross-legged position. It sat in a circular symbol that had been drawn onto the wooden floorboards, marked out in white chalk, though from this distance James couldn't see what the symbol was exactly. What he could see, however, was that this corpse had once been female—an elderly female, with sagging breasts and loose, wrinkled skin covered in cuts and markings. Again, this body had been supported by wooden sticks to hold its position—the left hand was set on top of something in its lap, and the right was held up to its side, bent at the elbow. James had no idea what the woman would have looked like in life, however, given that the head—or the original head—had been removed and replaced by that of a horned, black goat, and stitched at the neck.

Then he saw that the thing resting in the disgusting figure's lap was a head, and considered that it could be the original. But he soon saw that was not the case, because the face that stared back in open-mouthed horror was male, and one he recognised.

The question of whether Tony was alive or dead had finally been answered.

26

KEN FELT ALL the energy and hope drain from him.

He stepped slowly into the macabre surroundings of the church, his boots splashing in puddles of blood as he moved between the bodies, which were posed like marionettes in the middle of horrific acts. The fact that most of these corpses didn't appear to be fresh, nor have any running wounds, made the presence of the blood on the floor and walls all the more confusing.

But then again, nothing about this scene made sense. Least of all the head of his friend settled into the lap of that monstrous effigy at the head of the church.

The sight was so shocking, seeing Tony's face etched in an eternal horror, that Ken felt numb—like his soul was shutting down. It was just too much to comprehend.

Still, he continued to walk towards it. Because he had to know more. After all, Ken had been called here by a voice that had been so very dear to him—one he knew well. However, he had not found Amy inside as he'd hoped, but rather, this hellish display.

He should have known better. Of course Amy wasn't here—what the hell had he really expected to find?

Then again, perhaps what he saw all around him was not real at all, and that head in the lap of the posed goat-thing was not really not Tony's. James had been right before: this village should not exist, even before it had somehow changed locations. So maybe what Ken was being shown now was fake, or perhaps just a symptom of a shared madness they were all suffering from.

Somehow, though, he did not think that was the case.

Ken reached the goat-headed corpse and looked at the crude stitching at the neck. The stench the figure gave off actually overpowered the smell of decay elsewhere inside the building, reminding him of the stench that had seeped from the well outside. Ken knelt down, holding his breath, and looked closer at the head of his friend as it nestled in its resting place near the bare groin of the corpse.

Tony's jaw hung open slightly, and his wide eyes stared ahead, the pupils dulled with some kind of milky coating. The man's neck ended in a jagged stump, and vibrant red flesh was exposed, looking raw and fresh. A small pool of blood, now dried, had seeped from the wounds and trickled out beneath the goat-headed body, covering some of the symbol on the floor. Ken looked at that symbol closer now —the one the body was sitting centrally within—taking in the details. It was primarily formed by two large, concentric circles, and in between the circles were numerous, indecipherable markings. Lastly, the inner circle housed three more smaller rings, laid out in the shape of an inverted triangle, each split down the middle with a horizontal line.

In all his years of study of the macabre and the occult, Ken had never come across that symbol.

Ken then looked back to Tony's dead eyes and an overwhelming tidal wave of grief and guilt washed over him. Tears welled up and spilt from his eyes as he began to sob.

This whole fucking thing had been his fault.

He'd chosen the destination, he'd organised everything, and he was the one who hadn't listened when things started to go wrong—too focused instead on getting the answers he so desperately needed. But now, because of him, Tony was dead, Roberta's mind had broken, and they were now all stuck in an inescapable nightmare. One where the only escape seemed to be an impending death.

And even that, Ken realised, might not be the end.

As if to confirm this theory, Tony's milky eyes suddenly moved and focused on Ken. A horrible, drawn-out scream of anguish then erupted from the already open mouth.

'*Help me!*' Impossibly, the voice came from the decorated head. Its voice was strained, full of pain, and sounding somehow otherworldly—as if coming from a space removed from their reality. But still, Ken recognised the voice as Tony's. '*Please,*' his friend begged.

'Tony,' Ken replied, leaning forward. He had an impulse to reach out and take hold of the head, and even held out his arms to do so, but the thought of it was simply too much, too ghoulish, so he stopped. 'What happened? What can we do?' Ken asked.

'*I'm... in pain,*' Tony said, each word sounding like it was a struggle to get out. '*I can't... take it. This place... it's... hell. It's hell. Please... I'm begging you. Please... help me.*'

Another long scream, and then the face grew silent and lifeless again as the focus in the eyes fell away.

'Tony!' Ken screamed, now taking hold of the detached head and shaking it. 'Tony!'

Nothing.

He quickly realised what he was holding and let go,

allowing the head to drop to the floor where it landed with a thud, coming to a stop close to Ken's foot.

Ken took two paces back and stared with tears in his eyes at the horrible sight of what was left of his friend lying on the floor. Discarded, like an old mannequin head.

He then felt James' presence beside him.

'What the fuck was that?' James asked. 'Was it real?'

Ken could not answer him, and had no way of knowing. Not for certain. But he did feel that it was indeed his old friend communicating with him, from beyond this life, from a place that could be hell. And there was one thing Ken was now sure of.

'Tony's dead,' he stated. 'Whatever is behind all this, it has him now.'

'Can we help him?' James asked, his voice shaking.

Ken shrugged. 'I don't think so. I don't even think we can help ourselves.' He turned to look at the horrors around them, at the bodies that had been displayed. He wondered if they had once been presented like this in real life? Perhaps some kind or replay of events from the past.

Ken again turned to James. 'Where's Roberta?'

James took a moment to answer. 'Still outside, I think.'

'She didn't follow?'

James shook his head. 'No. And if I'm honest, I nearly didn't either.'

'Understandable,' Ken replied, feeling an urgent need to leave this place. He had clearly been summoned here, tricked with the voice of his daughter, but to what end? If more surprises lay ahead—beyond Tony's detached head talking to them—then Ken wanted no part of it. He'd been stupid to come here in the first place. 'We need to find Roberta, make sure she's okay.'

Ken was aware his voice sounded distant, because that's

how he felt—far away, somehow detached from reality. Perhaps he was close to his breaking point and would soon snap, as Roberta had.

'I'm not sure we do,' James said.

'What do you mean?'

'I don't think she's okay at all, and I really don't think we can trust her.'

'I know she's not coping well, James, but that's no reason—'

'That's not it!' James snapped, cutting in. 'Something is wrong with her. I don't think she's on our side anymore.'

'That's just because she can't handle what's happening to us,' Ken replied. 'Hell, I don't think I'm far off from losing it myself.'

'That isn't it,' James insisted. 'Roberta could get a little unnerved from time to time, sure, but she was as strong as any of us. This is something different. Something is in her head.'

'We don't know that.'

'But we do!' James argued. 'When you ran in here, Roberta told me that you would die in here. And she thought it was funny. She *wanted* it to happen. That's why I came. I thought I could catch you, but... I don't know, I'm not feeling right. I'm weak. Even now, I can barely stand. Something is happening to us, beyond all of the things we are seeing. Something from this forest is *inside us*.'

Ken considered what James was saying and, somewhere in the depths of his mind, it kind of made sense. But right now, after what had just happened, Ken was too overwhelmed to make sense of it all. Instead, he had to focus on more immediate issues.

'Let's get the hell out of here,' he said.

As soon as the words were uttered, however, the door to

the church slammed shut. At the same time, all of the candles simultaneously blew out.

'Holy shit!' James screamed.

Ken was shocked, too, of course, and not just because of the sudden darkness they had been plunged into. Just before the candles had blown out, Ken had seen a glimpse of movement from one of the corpses.

Low, guttural moans began to emanate around the two of them, accompanied by shuffling and scraping sounds.

'Jesus Christ,' Ken said, horror locking his body. 'I don't think these things are dead.'

27

WITH THE CANDLES out and the dull, flickering glow no longer illuminating the inside of the church, both James and Ken were plunged into near-complete darkness. Only the thin strips of sunlight that managed to seep between the gaps in the window boarding gave them any kind of visual aid at all.

But James didn't need to see anything to know that Ken was right. He could hear it. Sexualised moans of want and desire rose up like a terrible chorus, echoing off the stone walls all around them. What little light they had hinted at writhing movement, as the previously still and prone corpses were now animated.

James knew they were both now in imminent danger. He felt something take hold of his arm and was unable to stop from crying out in fright.

'It's me,' he heard Ken whisper, panic evident in the man's voice. 'We need to get out of here.'

An obvious statement—and one they had been using all too often recently—but a relevant one. 'The door,' James replied. 'We need to get to the main door.'

As far as he was aware, that was the only way in or out of the church, and they weren't able to look for another escape route.

Ken seemed to agree. 'Come on.'

He dragged James back in the direction they had come from as the sounds around them—groaning and the shuffling of movement—increased. The shards of light available to them acted as a guide to lead them back, helping them to make sure nothing barred their way. The pair had only taken a few dozen steps when something suddenly pulled itself into one of the spots of light, directly blocking their path. The two men pulled up short.

Most of the figure that barred their progress was shrouded in darkness, but from a sliver of light James could make out some of the details of its face as it pulled itself along the ground and through the beam of light. The eyes and mouth had been sewn shut, and around its throat was wrapped a dark purple strand of intestine, though it was unclear if the organ was its own or that of someone else. James didn't manage to see any more before it moved out of the light, but he could hear it slide across the floor towards them, now hidden by the darkness.

At the same time, other sounds converged from all around them: cries halfway between pain and pleasure, some muffled, some clear—all absolutely terrifying.

And then another noise rang out, a screaming that quickly rose above the incessant din of the undead. It was a voice, the one James and Ken had just heard, which in itself was maddening.

It was Tony.

And he was again screaming, '*Help me! Help me! Help me!*'

The panic, urgency, and pure desperation in the man's voice shook James, causing his fear levels to spike even higher, if that was possible. And then, James heard something else: a distinct bleating sound that was followed by a guttural, inhuman roar.

Suddenly, Tony's cries were cut off with a sickening, wet crunch. James didn't need to be able to see anything to know that the corpse that had been defiled with the head of a goat, and that had held Tony's decapitated head in its lap, was now up and moving as well. And it had stopped Tony's pleading.

James took off, unable to stop himself, with blind panic taking control of his actions. He knew the thing with the stitched-up eyes and mouth was still ahead, blocking his way, but he couldn't stand to be in that space anymore—he needed to be out of that fucking church, lest he meet a fate similar to Tony's.

'Damnit, James!' he heard Ken shout as managed to slip from the older man's grasp. As James sprinted off ahead, he felt his legs catch on something at the shin, and he toppled over the squirming mass before him, falling hard to the floor and cracking his forehead against something in the process.

After a moment, a sharp pain erupted, and he let out a groan as disorientation and nausea took over. He knew he needed to keep going, but at that moment James couldn't tell one way from another—which direction would take him to the door and which one would instead lead him back deeper into that hell. James then felt cold hands grab him. As the brief ringing in his ears faded away, he again heard a muffled but lustful moaning, this time right beside him. Whatever had hold of him then heaved itself on top of his grounded body. Though he tried to fight back, James' strength was sapped yet again, making him weak and useless. The flesh of the creature's groping hands felt cold and clammy, almost putty-like, and the smell that assaulted him—of rot and decay—was sharp and overwhelming. The weight was heavy, pinning James down, and he felt the dead hands grab at his trousers, trying to force them off while pulling at the belt. A renewed panic took over.

'Help!' he screamed. 'Ken! Help me!'

Thankfully, before the writhing corpse atop him could carry out whatever deed it intended, he felt another set of hands grab him by the shoulders and pull with considerable force, heaving James free of his captor. James managed to quickly climb back to his feet, but still felt the moving corpse grope at his legs.

'This way,' he heard Ken say, before being pulled along once again. James was happy to let Ken guide him this time, hoping his colleague knew the way to the door and could evade whatever other horrors lurked in the darkness.

The hungry noises followed them and closed in faster than James would have hoped, but it was impossible to tell how near the things that shambled after them were. Using the intermittent shafts of light, however, he could tell that he and Ken were getting closer to the exit. He just hoped it would open when they got there.

After a few more strides they crashed into the hard wood of the door and groped for the handle.

'Got it!' he heard Ken shout, filling him with relief. The door slowly heaved open and light from outside flooded in, allowing James, as he turned his head, to finally see what followed behind.

His heart sank, and he knew immediately that he would not make it. Ken rushed through the door, still holding James' arm, and tried to pull him through as well, but it was too late.

The writhing mass of bodies had been quicker than

James had expected and were already on him, multiple hands taking hold of his body. The writhing nightmares descended faster than they should have been able.

Ken looked back, and an expression of shock and horror quickly dawned across his face. His hold on James broke as James was heaved back by the nightmarish crowd, and the door between them was then forced shut, leaving him in darkness. The many creatures within pulled him to the floor as he screamed, pressing down on him and blocking off his air. He was unable to move—trapped beneath a hellish blanket of corpses.

James squirmed and screamed, but could do nothing to fight back against the overwhelming weight and mass of unseen terrors pinning him down.

Through the cacophony of lust, he then heard a distinctive sound.

One of laughter.

And it was not human.

28

KEN HAMMERED against the now-closed door to the church and pushed against it with all of his might.

'James! James!' he screamed, wildly.

But all he heard in response was those nightmarish sounds—horrible grunts and groans from inside, that radiated out even through the thick wood. He tried again to push against the entrance, throwing all of his weight into it, but the door was stuck fast, either blocked by those things on the other side or jammed in place by some other means. Perhaps the same thing that had opened the damn door in the first place, beckoning him inside, was now holding it shut and trapping James inside.

As Ken continued his futile pounding, desperate to help his friend, an unshakable feeling washed over him: the feeling that he was being watched. He turned his head and froze, seeing that the notion had indeed been correct.

The houses of the village—that had previously seemed abandoned—were now complete with figures standing in the open doorways. Upon focusing on these 'people,' Ken saw pale, twisted faces peeking back at him, both from the porches and also through the small windows.

He knew that this was the same mob of twisted, inhuman spectres that had blocked the group's escape from the forest earlier. Dressed in basic black-and-grey clothing, the male figures were wrapped in a mixture of dirty over-coats and linen shirts, while the women were donned in partlets, kirtles, and gowns, all of which reminded Ken—from his limited historical knowledge—of peasant clothing.

The majority of them looked thin and gaunt, and their limbs seemed almost elongated. The skin was pale and mottled, lined with dark purple lines of the veins that bulged beneath, and their faces were the thing of night-mares—Francis Bacon paintings come to life. Twisted and deformed, like a melted waxwork, with wild and glinting yellow eyes that peered back at him.

Looking at their demonic appearance was almost too much for Ken to bear, and he quickly pressed his back against the door behind him in fright—an involuntary reac-tion to what he had seen. His breath caught in his throat.

Though none of the watching crowd moved at all, most of them were smiling, and their mouths pulled unnaturally wide in animalistic glee. The teeth behind were a mixture of short, yellow stubs, or long, misshapen points, and even black, horse-like incisors. A thought then pulled itself up to the forefront of Ken's mind.

Roberta was nowhere to be seen.

Ken knew he needed to act, somehow, and wanted to turn back and continue to try and force open the door to the church. James was still inside and in great danger. But Ken did not dare turn his back on these townsfolk—if that was what they used to be—while they watched him. He had seen how quickly they could converge when his back was turned and did not want to let any of them out of his sight. Which meant that Ken was at an impasse—standing motionless, gazing upon the terrors that stared back, but not able to help James.

A movement to Ken's right drew his attention as a feminine figure stepped out from behind the church.

It was Roberta. And she looked worse than ever.

Her face and skin looked even closer to that of the demonic townsfolk than it was to the person who had entered this forest only a few days before. In addition, her eyes appeared sunken, and the smile she now wore was a horrible and malicious grin. Ken could see that many of the teeth behind her grin had blackened and a trail of black fluid, close to saliva in consistency, ran from her mouth, dripping from her chin.

'Hello, Ken,' she said, the words drawn out in a seductive tone that would have been more convincing had her voice not been so rough and strained. It didn't sound like Roberta speaking at all, but a sinister imposter. Which, Ken realised, might actually be close to the truth. She went on, 'So eager to get back inside, are you? That might be a mistake. I think the children in there are a little busy at the moment, so I'd take the reprieve while you can. But don't worry, Kenny-boy, Mother will make sure your turn comes around soon enough.' She let out a child-like giggle.

'What the hell is going on, Roberta?' Ken asked, on the verge on tears. His mind threatened to shatter into a thousand shards, given the terror and insanity of it all. 'Why are you being like this?'

Roberta laughed again and took a step towards him. 'Because I want to. I want to prove myself to my new family.' She then cast an arm out, gesturing farther into the depths of the village, towards the others present. Ken followed her movement, then gasped as he saw that the inhabitants of the cursed place had suddenly and silently grouped close to him, now standing only a few feet away.

'Get away from me!' Ken instinctively said and pressed himself farther into the door behind him in a futile bid to squirm away. But there was nowhere to go.

Roberta moved out before Ken and joined the things she had called her family, standing centrally among them. After she did, none of these demonic figures made a move towards her, instead happy to let her stand unharmed within their ranks.

And Ken understood at that moment that Roberta was truly one of them, and completely lost to him. How it all had happened, he could not comprehend, but that didn't change what he was clearly seeing, and Roberta smiled again, showing her blackened teeth.

'If you don't mind,' she said. 'We would like to go in there. Could you be a doll and get out of the way?'

She took a step forward, closer to Ken, and the mass of townsfolk around her moved as well. They didn't take a physical step as she had, but they came forward all the same —gliding from their original position and appearing closer to him, like they were somehow shifting through reality. Ken couldn't help but let out a scream.

He knew that James was still in danger inside the church, if he wasn't already dead. But Ken also realised that there was absolutely nothing he could do to help. He was overwhelmed. There were simply too many of these things —both out here and also inside.

And it was all part of the game, one where he and the others had been pawns. Pieces moved across the board at the whims of something above them. From the very start, the group had been toyed with and shepherded as needed, positioned like puppets by this Mother Sibbett and her master.

Ken realised that James was *meant* to be inside of that church right now. And, apparently, he was not.

Which, as Roberta had stated, gave him a reprieve, and a chance to perhaps escape from the madness—as long as he was prepared to leave James behind.

Was that something he was willing to do?

Ken reacted. He turned to his right and ran, sprinting as fast as he could away from the town, the church, and the demonic crowd, moving quickly out into the forest.

Clearly it *was* something he was willing to do: to leave behind a friend and colleague in order to save himself. Ken felt an immediate and heavy shame at his selfishness, but he did not stop.

While running, he looked back over his shoulder, expecting to see those things following him and appearing right behind him again, somehow both frozen in time yet still gaining ground.

That was not the case. He stopped and saw that the church door was open and the townsfolk were filtering inside in their unnatural, shifting manner. Roberta did not move, instead choosing to remain still, staring over to Ken. She was smiling. Only when the last of the entities around her disappeared inside of the old stone building did Roberta finally start to walk inside as well. Though as she did, Roberta kept her eyed focused directly on Ken and gave him a wave.

'See you soon!' she shouted before the heavy door swung shut behind her.

Ken was motionless, physically shaken at what had just transpired, unable to fully comprehend it. Roberta was one of them now. James had been right. And if James wasn't already dead, then he would be soon, likely sharing a similar fate to Tony.

One Ken would also share if he didn't act. That realisation gave him a much-needed kick, and Ken turned and once again took off running.

He picked no particular direction, however, his only concern getting as far away from that village as he could, leaving behind the things that resided there.

Things, he knew, that would be coming for him soon.

As he ran, Ken thought of James again, the man he'd left behind. A fresh wave of guilt swept over him.

You're useless, he thought to himself. *Incapable of saving anyone. First Tony, then James, and now Roberta, who was lost to this madness.*

You couldn't even save your own daughter.

What chance did he really have of saving himself? And as the air burned in his lungs, he had one other question he struggled to answer.

Was he even worth saving?

29

JAMES SLOWLY OPENED his eyes as he regained consciousness.

For a fleeting moment, he was in that state of complete unawareness where the mind had not yet retrieved the last of its memories, and he did not fully understand where he was or the situation he was in.

It was a blissful ignorance, but one that was all too brief.

Then it came crashing back to him. All of it: trying to flee the church. Being overcome by the shambling monstrosities within. The door closing in front of him, with Ken's horrified face being closed off. The pressure James felt as he was overwhelmed by those things. And, just before losing consciousness as his breath was cut off, the stark notion that Ken had not returned to help him.

As the room around James came into focus, he realised he was still in the church. The candles were lit once again, casting their eerie glow, and through the slight gaps in the boards over the windows he could see that night had fallen. And that meant he had been unconscious for a number of hours already.

Things only got worse as it became immediately clear

he was lying on the floor, completely bound. His arms and legs were splayed out to his sides like the Vitruvian Man, and he was tied by his hands, wrists, neck, and waist to a frame of thick wooden poles, all held together by twine and rope. From his limited view, James saw that the central column of the frame consisted of multiple shafts bound together, forming a thick column that ran the length of his body—from above his head to below his feet. From this central section, other thinner rods sprouted, at roughly forty-five-degree angles, supporting the splay of his arms and legs.

Despite his struggles against it, the star-like frame was far too sturdy to break, and James' bonds were too tight for him to wriggle free. He was stuck, unable to escape and—to his horror—completely naked.

And he was not alone.

Even though Ken had abandoned him, there were many other things present, and he screamed at the sight of them.

The undead monstrosities that had first been prone and displayed in disgusting positions before writhing to life were all there. They were motionless again, as they had been when James had first set foot inside, but they now stood around him, standing vigil, watching with glinting eyes.

Others were present, too, but were different. Though they were fully clothed, they didn't seem any more human and had twisted, nightmarish faces, and expressions that yearned for him. At the centre of them all, however, was someone else. Someone he knew. The sight of her there amongst all of the madness was almost too much for him to take.

It was the woman he loved. Or at least she used to be. He wasn't sure what she was anymore. She certainly looked a lot different now—a shell of her former vibrant and beautiful self.

'Roberta!' he shouted, hearing a pathetic pleading tone in his own voice. 'What's happening?'

She took a step forward, carrying an expression that bordered somewhere between lust and hate.

'Best not to talk,' she said in a horrible, gravelly voice. 'No one will listen. And nothing can stop what is going to happen to you. *She* wills it, and therefore it will come to pass. But I will say this...' Roberta knelt down beside him, holding up a dirtied length of once-white material. 'If you let yourself relax, there is a chance you might get some enjoyment out of this. At least, to start with.'

'Please let me go,' James whimpered, but Roberta just tittered and caressed his cheek.

'That isn't going to happen. But, luckily for you, we do get to have a parting present. One last expression of passion before you make your journey. So, if I were you, I'd give myself over. Enjoy what you can... *while* you can.'

She then moved beside him, to her knees, with the length of material in one hand. James understood it to be a blindfold, and she hovered it above him as her other hand made its way down to his crotch. James' body locked at her gentle touch—her hands ice cold—and he let out an involuntary gasp.

'Please, Roberta, I'm begging you,' he said. His voice cracked as tears started to come.

'Oh,' Roberta replied, leaning in closer still. 'You haven't even started to beg yet. But you will.'

Roberta then took a firm hold of his penis and gave it a squeeze, before rhythmically massaging it with her cold palm and fingers. She giggled again and James felt his own body betray him as his dick began to stiffen. He couldn't understand how that was possible given the terror that surged through him, as well as the physical condition of Roberta herself. She now looked far beyond just being sick. She instead appeared to be at death's door.

Or, more accurately, she had already crossed the threshold.

And yet, with her confident manipulations, she was able to turn him on, at least part of him—the part that counted —while in the middle of the nightmarish situation.

'Roberta, stop,' he said, trying to sound forceful but failing miserably. James writhed and squirmed within her grasp in an attempt to move his groin away from her playful, mottled hand, though his efforts were useless. James still felt so weak that he doubted Roberta even needed the restraints to overpower him.

'You know,' she said as she worked, 'we actually know very little about sex and desire. We might think we do— humanity has an arrogant way of thinking it knows everything—but we don't. However, Mother Sibbett and her chosen few have found a way to take our carnal urges and use them in a much more meaningful way. Because, as it turns out, we were right about this place—you, me, Ken, and Tony. We were right about the Black Forest. There *is* something here. Something far older than we can imagine. Mother Sibbett was the first to serve this great, old power, and because of that, she was granted insight. And she was able to spread a new Gospel, an inversion to God and Christ, only it was something far more real. And one of the ways it was done was by indulging their most basic desires. Did you know that? We just give in to our most depraved urges, instead of stifling and hiding them as we've been taught in life. We need to become one with ourselves, our real selves, not the acts we put on in front of others. The masks we wear need to slip away to find true enlightenment.'

Roberta's hands started to work faster, causing James to shift uncomfortably in her grip again. She briefly stopped, but only long enough to wrap the blindfold over his eyes, as she had the night before.

Yet again, James tried to fight, this time to move his head out of the way, but the bond around his neck made that impossible.

'Let me go, Roberta,' James pleaded again. With the blindfold secured, James' vision left him in complete darkness, but he heard excited murmurs fill the room from the demonic audience.

Roberta continued her teasing, still keeping him unwillingly erect.

'Are you ready?' she asked him.

30

Ken's body was a fire of aches and pains.

He sat on the still-wet ground, his back propped up against a fallen tree, and tried desperately to catch his breath. Night had now set in, reducing his visibility drastically, and he had an unshakable feeling that there were things out there in the dark waiting for him to wander close. And it terrified him.

He'd pushed himself as hard as he could all day, not stopping once, keeping up as fast a pace as possible. However, such effort over an extended period of time had truly taken it out of him.

After fleeing the town—leaving James to his fate—Ken had run for about fifteen minutes straight over the rough and uneven terrain, putting as much distance between himself and that God-forsaken place as he possibly could. It was only then that he changed direction and bore back towards what he thought was the edge of the forest—the same direction they'd all been going before those things had shown up and stopped the group in their tracks.

But, in reality, Ken had no idea if he was heading in the

right direction or not—his bearings were shot. He was so disorientated that even using the compass left him unsure of the correct route. He still had his backpack with him—given he hadn't taken it off all day—which included his tent and provisions. But now, as he sat struggling to catch his breath, Ken considered ditching some of his gear. He'd need to keep his food and water if he had any hope of survival, of course, but his tent and sleeping bag... were they really essential?

Ken had no plans to stop and sleep that night, not after what he'd seen earlier, regardless of how tired and exhausted he felt. Instead, he aimed to push on, continuing until he broke free of the forest or his body failed him and he dropped—whichever came first.

Indeed, there was no way he could sleep now anyway, not after Roberta's warning that he was running on borrowed time. She, and the forces that she seemed to have aligned with, would be coming for him as soon as they were done with James.

If they weren't already.

The guilt at leaving his friend—and at his own cowardice and selfishness—never left him, weighing on his psyche. He couldn't get the thought of James' shocked expression from his mind, the one he'd seen just before the door of the church closed and James understood he would be left behind. On some level, Ken knew that he could have done nothing to save his friend. There was no way he could ever have gotten that door open—Lord knows he tried. But even if he had, that only meant he would now be inside with James and the horrors that had filtered in with Roberta.

But shouldn't he have at least tried? Even sacrificed himself in an attempt?

While Ken was aware that survivor's guilt was a thing, he

knew this was different. For one thing, he hadn't survived yet. And for another, he knew that this whole thing was his fault. He'd brought them out here to meddle in things that they had no business being around.

His past experiences with Tony and the others, and even before when he'd investigated on his own, had been nothing, he now knew. If anything supernatural had taken place during those searches, then the events were so fleeting and minuscule as to have been inconsequential. However, though he had always demanded hard evidence, in truth every little thing had given him hope and fuelled him in his quest for the truth.

But now, after experiencing the Black Forest, it put everything else into perspective.

Ken had started the whole Paranormal Encounters endeavour with a yearning to understand if there really was a life after death. Because he so dearly needed to know there was more to this existence than this fleeting life.

Well, he had his answer now, but what the Black Forest had shown him was not what he'd hoped for. The afterlife, at least here, seemed a place of nightmares and never-ending torment of the soul.

Was this the kind of existence his little girl now experienced? Was all the afterlife reminiscent of the horrors he'd witnessed here?

Or was this place somehow different?

Ken forced his mind back to more immediate concerns and slipped off his rucksack. He pulled the tent free, including the supporting poles, and also discarded his sleeping bag, leaving them in a heap on the ground.

If Ken did need to rest in the coming hours, then he would just have to drop and sleep where he fell. Because if it came down to it, and he wasn't out of this forest by the time his legs gave out, then he knew he would never leave.

After shedding the items and equipment he'd deemed to be excess weight, Ken heaved himself up to his feet and trudged on, walking into the darkness while hoping he was heading in the right direction.

And he prayed that he would break free of the forest before the demons that lurked turned their attention back to him.

31

EXCITEMENT PERMEATED throughout the room as the things that watched James started to intensify their murmurs and groaning. He could only hear them, given his ability to see had been cut off, but he noticed that the sounds grew closer, and were accompanied by shuffling.

They were closing in.

Roberta released her grip on him, leaving James alone, feeling horribly exposed as he still lay on the floor, bound to the frame. Giddy wails then emanated from the gathered crowd, becoming louder and more aggressive. James tensed up, not knowing what to expect, and detected movement over him.

Roberta, he knew.

James then felt the girl mount him, slipping herself onto his engorged penis, forcing herself down. He groaned in discomfort, her rough dryness making the motion uncomfortable. Roberta then began to gyrate as a foul smell assaulted him.

James knew that Roberta had changed—both physically

and mentally—but the decaying smell that completely engulfed his senses proved just how much her former self was now lost. This thing that sat atop him was something else entirely.

It was one of them—if not entirely, then it was very close.

Roberta's thrusting soon began to increase, getting faster and faster and rubbing James raw as he fought against her. However, given how dry and coarse Roberta's sex felt, the friction became intensely painful.

'Stop!' he screamed, drawing more noises of approval from the watchers around him, who all seemed to take glee in his protests.

A hand then covered his mouth and pressed hard over his lips. The surface of the palm—while cold—was different than what James had expected; it didn't feel like skin, as much as rough, scaly leather. The hand then moved, and he felt a finger dip into his mouth, plunging into his throat, causing James to gag. Again, the finger that violated him did not seem normal, as when his lips involuntarily clenched around it the digit felt thin, almost skeletal, and far too long. James then felt a long nail scratch at the back of his throat, and he began gagging and coughing more severely.

Undeterred by his fighting, Roberta continued bouncing atop him, her motions becoming quicker and more frantic. And despite the pain he was feeling, her movement was somehow still keeping him excited, driving him towards a climax.

How can I get excited at this?

It was maddening that his body could betray him so much, that his libido could still hold firm in the face of such disgusting horror. Finally, the finger pulled free of his mouth, and James turned his head to the side. Instinctively retching he purged the contents of his stomach across the floor.

'Let me go!' he demanded after he'd finished, trying to sound more assertive this time. But it did no good—he knew it wouldn't. They were not going to let him go. His girlfriend —the woman who rode him at that very moment—wanted him dead, served up to nightmarish demons.

The noises around James—excitable grunts and groans of the crowd, who seemingly approved of the gross act they were watching—continued to rise. Roberta, however, made no sound at all as she continued to sexually assault him. She didn't even seem to be breathing heavily, which was a stark difference to the previous night when she had been incredibly vocal.

He felt Roberta lean closer to him, shifting her position while still keeping him inside of her. James felt her face hover above him, and suddenly felt her mouth on his.

Her tongue invaded his mouth, thrashing around inside and lapping at his own, before pushing farther in. The appendage was withered and shrivelled, feeling like a crusty vine... and it kept going, wriggling down into his throat before slowly drawing back and then dropping once more, the length of the thing completely unnatural. Roberta's mouth was pressed tightly to his, but James could feel no lips, only gums and teeth. He fought desperately, fearful of choking on the probing tongue, but could do nothing to resist. Tears flowed freely as James could only lie there and accept what was happening to him.

He had been terrified before, but now his panic and fear reached new heights.

Then James heard a voice, one that was distinct to him, and it came from a few feet behind him.

'Don't resist it, James,' it said. 'Let her have her way.'

James' body seized as he recognised the voice to be Roberta's.

But if she was standing away from him, then that meant the person currently thrusting on top of him was not her.

Ice ran through his veins, and his squirming and fighting resumed with renewed energy, desperate to stop the unknown thing that writhed atop him.

As if reading his mind, the tongue slithered its way out of his mouth, allowing much-needed air to once again enter his lungs. James coughed and spluttered, fighting not to vomit again when the blindfold was quickly ripped away from his head. As his vision restored, James let out a long, panicked scream.

What he saw above him was far more terrifying than anything he'd seen in his entire life.

Though, in truth, he had seen glimpses of this woman before, in the video footage taken on their first night in the Black Forest. At the time, however, she had been peeping from behind a tree, teasing her presence, only half of her face on display. That had been an unsettling image, but now he was able to take everything in, eliciting a repulsion that sickened James to his core.

The woman was not human.

James was now staring up to the cold, dead form of Mother Sibbett.

Her long black hair was thin and greasy and hung down to her midsection, but it was so damp that it clung in clumps to light brown, brittle skin that had the consistency of dried meat. The ghoulish woman's frame was painstakingly thin and frail; her ribs and collarbone stretched the flesh to the point of splitting, and her stomach was sunken so much that it almost reached the spine behind. Her hands—that now lowered and started to caress James' chest—had long, spindly fingers, and they ran to a claw-like point at the ends. The face was a mangled, distorted mess of features: sagging eyes, and a mouth that looked painfully too wide and also revealed long, razor-sharp teeth behind. The shape of Mother Sibbett's skull was evident as the skin that pulled tightly over it clung to the bone like lycra. Mother Sibbett's gross appearance was rounded off with a long, twisted nose that ended in a definite hook.

But as bad as all of that was, there was one feature in particular that truly terrified James, and it was the one most evident, too, covering the entirety of her form: multiple rolling eyes lined her body like tumours. Some clustered together in groups, like globs of caviar, while others were dotted intermittently about the expanse of flesh. Each fleshy orb, complete with a jet-black pupil, looked about wildly, flitting in different directions and all moving independently.

And James' quickly deflating penis was still inside this horror.

He continued his wild, manic screaming and bucking, trying to throw the demonic witch off, but it was useless. He then saw Roberta approach and kneel at his head.

'Fun's over,' she told him. 'Things are about to get a little... painful.'

And they did.

The claws at his midsection suddenly thrust down, piercing his flesh at the stomach and pulling it open. Agony flared, and James' cries echoed off the stone walls around them.

And then his suffering began in earnest, and Mother Sibbett bestowed upon him acts of torture and deviancy that completely broke his mind.

The baying crowd of monstrosities around him then descended to partake in the fun as well. One of the last things James saw was the gleeful face of Roberta as she indulged her deviancy to the fullest.

32

KEN CHECKED HIS WATCH.

He'd been walking again for a little over two hours, and it was now close to one in the morning. Since he'd discarded his tent and sleeping bag, moving through the forest had become a little easier. However, that didn't change the fact that he was still bordering on exhaustion. As much as he didn't want to stop, Ken couldn't force his aching body on any farther and dropped down to a sitting position. He took off his pack and rechecked the compass to make sure he was heading west—the direction he hoped would take him out of the forest. After confirming that was indeed the case, he set the instrument down on top of his rucksack.

He was tired. *Soooo fucking tired.*

So he lay back, stretching out across a patch of soft ground that felt damp. He could smell the musty wet grass and soil, since it was now only inches from his nose, but he didn't care. He didn't have the energy to care.

Though his thermal clothing kept Ken warm, he knew that if he were to lie in place for long, the biting cold would soon become difficult to bear. Of course, that would make drifting off to sleep difficult, which was a good thing.

He didn't want to sleep. Couldn't afford to.

But he did want rest, and just needed a little longer.

Ken yet again thought of James, certain that his friend was now dead, probably sharing a similar fate to Tony's. Both of them had died because of him. And then there was Roberta... and he had no idea what to even make of that. She might not be dead, at least physically, but after what he'd seen of her, Ken couldn't be sure there was anything left of the Roberta he knew. Not anymore.

And that left only him.

Ken realised he was crying, and he noticed his first instinct was to stop himself, to swallow the guilt and the pain—emotions he knew all too well—and to push them down inside of himself. Because he could ill afford to let himself lose control and potentially draw the attention of the things that lived in the forest.

But he couldn't.

The tears came anyway, strong and quick, and soon he was a sobbing mess. Through clouded thoughts of Tony, James, and Roberta, another figure ghosted its way to the forefront of his thoughts.

Amy.

Ken cried for her most of all as the familiar pain took hold. It was an agony he lived with every day, one that existed just below the surface of his fake exterior—a horrible constant—and it now overwhelmed him. If the guilt of Tony's and James' deaths had been tough, and it was, then it paled in comparison to the grief and responsibility he felt over the death of his daughter.

She had been only eight years old when it happened. Far too young to have experienced the things she had. That had been a little over ten years ago, meaning she would have been a young adult now.

But that life had been taken from her, snatched away cruelly and violently, in a way that made Ken certain there could be no God. Because what sort of merciful God could possibly have allowed that to happen someone so innocent?

So no, God wasn't to blame for what had happened to Amy.

Ken was.

He'd been with her. He'd let her out of his sight for the brief moment it took for his world to fall apart. And he was the one who had so utterly failed in his responsibilities as a parent.

He could almost hear her voice now, almost remembered how she called to him in that terrible moment before it all happened.

Ken had been talking on his mobile phone, when he should have been paying more attention, as the two of them walked through the bustling town centre, weaving between the throng of the crowd as they moved. Ken had been running late. He hadn't wanted Amy with him that day, anyway, as he'd had an important meeting to attend. Though it should have been a low-key affair—coffee with an agent to talk about his book—it'd still had the potential to change his life. But Ken's wife had been called into work, leaving him in charge of their daughter. Thankfully, he'd managed to get the okay from the agent to bring Amy along and so had taken her with him, walking as fast as they could across the footpath, Ken desperate not to be even a minute late. But that had looked unlikely, given there had been an accident on the surrounding roads that had caused the traffic to back up. By the time he had managed to get parked, Ken had less than five minutes to spare before the meeting was due to start. So Ken had set off running, with Amy in tow, rang the agent on his mobile —the man who held the keys to the kingdom—and apologised profusely.

Then he remembered hearing Amy let out a grunt. He turned, just in time to see her fall into the road, accidentally nudged by a passerby. She had been going so fast that, when hit, the young girl couldn't keep her balance. She had then looked up in horror as the truck, with no chance to stop, hurtled towards her. And Ken had then heard her final words as her eyes darted over to him.

Daddy.

He should have been there for her. Should have saved her. He should have paid more fucking attention.

Instead, he had frozen, and he remembered the expression on Amy's face just before the truck hit. That realisation that her father, the man she looked up to, the man who was supposed to make everything better, couldn't help her. A look of realisation that her daddy was going to fail her when it counted most.

Ken wailed harder and hugged himself, the memory real and raw. He hated reliving it, but did so every night, either when awake or by way of his tortured subconscious as he slept.

After that day, Ken's life had truly fallen apart. He and his wife could not get past what had happened—he never blamed her for that—so he withdrew from the world, finding solace in the only thing he could: the hope that somewhere, somehow, Amy was able to live on.

Because if that were possible then maybe, just maybe, the crushing guilt that had grown to be part of his life could finally ease, if only a little. And perhaps he could then see her again one day, and he would have the chance to tell Amy that he loved her and that he was so very sorry about what had happened.

And he would beg and plead for her forgiveness.

Daddy.

The voice was so real, as if it were coming through the trees on the wind and not just from Ken's own tortured thoughts.

'*Daddy.*'

He then paused his sobbing and his eyes slowly opened wide. A feeling halfway between fear and amazement surged through him as he realised that the words he'd heard hadn't been in his head.

They had been real.

Ken turned his head to the left, to the source of the sound, and froze, unable to believe what he saw. He was already crying, but that only intensified and tears flooded his eyes once again. He began to shake, unable to process the vision of his daughter standing out between the trees in the darkness.

Somewhere, a voice inside told him that this wasn't reality, and that his daughter wasn't really there with him. Something else was behind what he was seeing right now, and that something had already proved itself to be absolute evil.

And yet the sight of the little girl—still dressed in the denim dungarees she had worn on that fateful day—was so powerful that it overrode all logic.

'Amy?' he asked, his voice a whisper.

Please be true, please be true, please be true.

The small girl nodded, then began to walk forward, her dirty blonde hair swaying in its pigtails as she moved. Her face was just as he remembered it: with cherubic red cheeks, innocent and full brown eyes, and a slightly buttoned nose.

'Amy, is that really you?'

She giggled. The sound was so real, so genuine, and so raw that it broke Ken down and cut right to his heart.

It was her laugh.

'*Of course it's me, Daddy,*' she said, her voice almost as he remembered it.

Almost.

There was a slight rasp to it that he hadn't known before, as well as having an echoey quality to it.

'*You're silly,*' she went on and giggled again. The girl walked closer to him, stopping only a few feet away.

'I'm so sorry,' he said to her, desperate to get the words out. She needed to know how much he regretted failing her, and that not a day went by he didn't think of her.

'*Sorry for what?*' she asked, cocking her head. Then blood ran from her nose. '*Sorry for killing me?*'

A horrible feeling began to worm around in Ken's gut, and he could only watch on in alarm as her very form changed before him. Bones cracked, an arm splintered, and her body twisted into horrible, painful positions. Cuts and gashes developed over her skin and a dent formed in her skull.

'Amy?'

She walked forward again, her movements now awkward and broken as she heaved her twisted legs in laboured steps. '*Sorry for ignoring me? For caring more about your meeting than my life? Sorry for not trying to save me? Is that what you're sorry about, Daddy?*'

Ken got to unsteady feet and moved back. Amy continued to approach. The sight of her in this condition turned his stomach, but also unlocked something deep within him that pushed Ken to the breaking point. He'd always remembered Amy on that fateful day, but had forced himself to think of her as she was before the accident.

What had remained of her body after, he had blocked out, so painful was the memory.

But now that memory was in front of him, and it hobbled closer, showing him exactly what he'd done to his beloved daughter.

'I'm sorry,' he whimpered again. 'I'm so sorry, Amy.'

'*Not good enough!*' she snapped and continued towards him. Ken backpedaled, matching her pace, something inside telling him he had to keep away. He turned his head, as looking at her broken form was just too painful. '*Saying sorry is not good enough. Look at me!*'

He didn't want to. It was just too hard. 'What do you want me to do?' he asked. 'Please, just tell me and I'll do it.'

She laughed, and the sound was not the sweet and innocent one of moments ago. This was laced with malice.

'*I want to you stay here,*' she said. '*Stay in this forest, Daddy. Stay here with Mother Sibbett. Let her take you. She'll make you real sorry, I promise you. Then I'll know you regret what you did. And I'll know that, deep down, you do really love me, because you'll have accepted what you deserve. Will you do that for me, Daddy? Will you stay here with her?*'

She began to laugh again—that horrible, mocking sound. Ken turned and ran, sprinting away from the nightmarish vision that taunted him as he fled.

He'd known that thing couldn't have been his daughter, but after seeing her, as she was, as she used to be, the temptation and need to believe was just too overwhelming.

But it had been nothing more than a cruel trick. And it had pushed him to the brink, as right now there was a strong temptation to simply lie down and let the monsters of the forest take him and dish out their punishment, one that he so richly deserved. Because even if that thing behind him wasn't Amy, what it had said to him rang true.

Because you'll have accepted what you deserve.

For now, though, he ran. Farther into the woods, knowing he would soon meet his fate, one way or the other. The only question was, did he even want to survive?

KEN WANDERED the forest until dawn broke, unable to get any bearings on which way he was going. He'd left his pack behind after running from the vision of his daughter, meaning he was without food and water, and also without his compass.

He was completely alone—isolated like a stray doe—and had nothing but the clothes on his back to protect him from the elements. His body was ravaged with exhaustion, but it also craved food and—more importantly—water.

Though the sky above was starting to brighten, the sun had not yet reached a high-enough level to break over the canopy of the trees that surrounded him. Once it did, he hoped he would be able to work out which direction he was travelling. Perhaps that could help him get back on track. But for the moment, his walking was aimless and without purpose, merely moving for the sake of it, to keep the horrors within the forest at his back rather than out in front.

With his throat dry and coarse, and his body craving refreshment, Ken made sustenance an immediate priority, though he had no idea where that would come from. His first thought was to find a stream or brook, but he couldn't remember seeing a single one in all the time he'd been in the Black Forest. His next idea was to check the leaves of plants and trees, to see if any rainwater residue was still there that could be harvested. He found only droplets, which he greedily slurped up—moving from one leaf to the next, getting all he could. It amounted to less than a mouthful in total, but at least it was something. Enough to wet his mouth, but a far cry from satisfying his thirst.

Ken even contemplated going back to retrieve his rucksack. There he had water left, and even food, that would help give him the energy he needed to keep going. But he knew what would be waiting for him back there, as he hadn't been able to shake it from his mind. And he didn't think he was strong enough ever to see that again.

So he ruled out the idea.

He knew the chance of finding food out in the woods was likely non-existent, given he knew nothing about the plant life of the forest, nor its edibility. So that meant turning his attention to the wildlife that resided in these woods.

The thought of catching and cooking an animal over a fire seemed incredibly difficult, if not impossible, but he knew it was something he would need to seriously consider soon. For now, however, he searched more of the vegetation for further droplets of precious water. As he did, he contemplated his fatalistic thinking of the previous night, where he had questioned his worthiness to live. In truth, that internal battle was still unresolved, but for now, at least, an inherent drive for survival had taken hold and was pushing him on.

But he could feel that fading.

Ken's weariness, coupled with the hopelessness of his situation, threatened to kill whatever urge he had to survive. And, in truth, whether he wanted it or not, Ken could not see a scenario where he made it out of the forest alive. Not when he considered what it was that hunted him.

Which led him to think about the legend of the Black Forest, and how much of it he, or the others, had now witnessed for themselves.

Back before Roberta had lost her mind, she had claimed to have seen the fabled Mother Sibbett. Indeed, Ken had seen evidence of her himself on the recording Roberta had taken. And he had also seen the very village thought to have been lost to the ages, or at least a version of it—one that was presented to him. And he had seen the souls of the damned that still lived in that village. If 'living' was even the correct term for it.

None of the things he'd seen were natural, and they didn't belong to this world, especially not when they were driven by such malevolence and malice.

Ken understood now that this evil had preyed upon people exactly like him—drawing them into a nightmare from which they would never escape. And he also knew that it was unlikely he would ever gain any true understanding of what it was he faced; he would only be shown what the unknowable entity wanted him to see.

Ken's mission over the past ten years had been to reveal the existence of the paranormal. Well, he had achieved that. But how he wished he could just continue on in blissful ignorance again.

He regretted ever hearing the name of the Black Forest all those years ago. And the realisation of how long this place had been a part of his life shocked him, with the story revealing itself to him at an early age, and helping to spark his interest in the paranormal. Ken wondered if his fate had been determined, even back then. Was the reach of the forest able to stretch back through time itself?

Ken gave pause as the thought continued to run and develop. Could the forest—and, by extension, the presence that lived here—have even been behind the death of his daughter? Perhaps it was also responsible for his subsequent dive into a quest for the truth. All of it could just have been part of a decades-long plan, put in motion in his youth when the first story was told to him, all with the goal of one day drawing him back here.

He shook his head. *Preposterous.*

The notion was just the product of a tired and weary mind, one that was close to being broken. There was no way the course of his life could have been determined back then.

Was there?

No, surely not. The only thing that brought him here was bad fucking luck—horrible circumstances that had not played in his favour—and right now he needed to keep his head, not let himself spiral deeper into despair.

Ken spent the rest of the morning and early afternoon continuing to push on. Eventually, the sun peeked over the trees, and he was able to orient himself. It rose in front of him, which meant—he was sure—that he had to walk away from it in order to head back west.

But did he really want to go that way? Every time they had tried that route before, something had happened to stop their escape, and he doubted it would be any different if he tried again.

Another option was to instead try and push on ahead and go east, breaking out on the other side of the forest. Hell, he could even turn ninety-degrees and try north or south. This place couldn't stretch on forever.

Problem was, he didn't know which way, other than

west, was the shortest route.

But then, did it even matter? Even if he picked a direction and stuck to it, did he really expect safe passage straight out of this place?

Of course not.

But he was out of options, and he had to do something. He could either keep trying to escape until that proved physically impossible or just drop down and give up completely.

He wasn't ready for that yet. Not quite.

But he didn't know how much longer the slim resolve would hold out.

So he walked east, hoping that way would turn out to be more successful, but knowing deep down it wouldn't.

Hours passed, and Ken's aching for food increased. He felt drained and weak. His body had started to tremble, and dizzy spells became frequent. When a particularly bad one hit, Ken stopped and leaned against a tree, giving himself time to recuperate. Seconds stretched to minutes before the latest bout of dizziness passed.

Ken knew he needed nourishment quickly if he expected to go on.

Then, as if God had heard his desperation, something hopped through the undergrowth ahead, displacing the grass and shrubbery and moving quickly towards him before finally breaking through the high grass. Ken remained as still as possible the whole time, and he saw a small brown rabbit bound into view. It then stopped, its little nose twitching and large, round eyes on high alert.

The animal looked extremely cute and cuddly, and Ken hated what he was about to try to do. But he had no choice. He needed to dig deep if he wanted to survive.

Given there were only a few feet between him and the

rabbit, Ken felt he had a decent chance of catching the animal if he timed his attack just right. It continued to smell the air, but did not move. If the small creature knew Ken was there, then it did not seem scared by his presence.

So he readied himself, his mind already running ahead to try and work out the best way to light the fire that would cook this animal. Ken had never tasted rabbit before, but at that moment anything would taste like a five-star meal to him.

Ken held his breath... and lunged. But it was useless.

The rabbit quickly turned and leapt back into the undergrowth—with amazing speed and agility—before Ken had even taken a few steps. He gave chase, scrambling after the fleeing animal, but the rabbit was simply too quick, and it made good its escape. While the small creature may have been frightened, in truth Ken had come nowhere near catching it, so feeble was his attempt. He dropped to his knees and cursed.

He should have known. Nothing would go his way while in these cursed woods. There was only evil and torment here. And it wouldn't have shocked him if that animal revealing itself was just another way for Mother Sibbett to wear him down even more—by dangling a thread of hope, only to yank it away.

Ken's hunger continued to gnaw at his gut, to the point where it was becoming painful. The action of heaving himself back up to his feet took a lot more effort than it should have, and he walked forward on unsteady steps.

He knew he couldn't keep this up much longer.

The rest of the day passed in a similar vein for him, with Ken heading due east in order to get clear of the forest. But his progress was painfully slow given his weakened state, and hunger, thirst, and fatigue were all starting to take their terrible toll on him. Ken spied other animals over the course of the day, all potential meals, but he had no more success catching those than he had the rabbit.

A huntsman, it turned out, he was not.

As darkness set in his apprehension grew, and he wondered what horrors would lie in store for him that night, or if he would even survive it. The final light was eventually taken and stars pin-pricked the sky. Ken trudged on for an hour more in the dark before he heard it: something approaching from behind. Whatever was coming was clearly much bigger than a rabbit, or any other forest animals he had seen. Signalled by the sounds of thumping footsteps hitting grass and bare patches of dirt, the unknown pursuer was moving quickly... and gaining ground steadily.

Whatever it was, Ken heard it break into a sprint.

Thump, thump, thump, thump.

Ken's heart-rate quickened and he, too, set off running. His stride, however, was slow and laboured as he struggled to navigate in the dark. It was clear to him that whoever was giving chase was rapidly gaining ground on him.

Quicker and quicker the footsteps became, and at last Ken turned around to look behind, and he saw what it was.

The woman broke into view, moving as fast and quick as an animal, hitting speeds that should have been impossible for a human being.

It was Roberta.

At least, it had been once. The sight of her now chilled Ken to his core, causing his heart to beat even faster— reaching dangerous levels of palpitations. Fiery pain shot down his left arm.

'Oh, Ken!' Roberta screamed in a voice that sounded more demon than feminine. 'I've come to play!'

34

SHE WAS on him in an instant, tackling Ken to the ground with frightening ease. He felt an acute pain flare up in the small of his back as the tender muscle struck something beneath him when he fell.

Ken struggled to get air into his body, and his heart went into overdrive, beating out of rhythm while the pain in his left arm increased, shooting up and down. The best he could do was to suck in short, sharp breaths.

He wasn't a doctor by any means, but Ken knew something was very wrong, though he had no idea how severe it was. And the knowledge that something beyond his control was happening to him only served to panic him more.

And, of course, it did not help to be looking up at Roberta's ruined body while she sat mounted on his prone form.

The once-beautiful woman had changed now almost beyond recognition. Her skin was the consistency of dried tree bark, with deep lines running between flat, wart-like lesions. Her sunken eyes appeared cloudy in the pits of her sockets, but had that ominous yellow gleam to them that Ken had seen on the other entities back at the church. The few strands of hair she still possessed had lost their colour, and were now a lifeless grey. On top of all that, the woman was now completely naked, and Ken could see that, in some areas, dark spots had formed at the head of some of the fleshy, puss-filled lumps that covered her body. These dark spots moved around in a murky liquid, like tadpoles still in their sacks.

She stunk, too. The musty, rotten stench that seeped from her pores was enough to make Ken gag as he struggled for air.

'Having a little trouble there, Ken?' Roberta asked, her voice now a grotesque, hoarse rasp, as if the inside of her throat was as dry and hard as the surface of her skin. 'Breathing a little difficult?' She laughed. The mocking noise her throat created sounded old... even ancient.

Ken couldn't reply, as he had no breath in his lungs to do so. All he could do was try and fight what was happening to his body—forcing himself to calm down and slow his heart rate. But the nightmarish situation he was in was not conducive to anything but panic.

Roberta dropped her head towards him and curled the edges of her lips up into a sneer. 'Want me to administer CPR?'

Her black and lumpy tongue then snaked from her mouth and smeared over her bottom lip. The thick, viscous saliva that ran from the inside of her mouth was black as well, giving the appearance that Roberta had been guzzling tar.

But instead of carrying through with her threat of mouth-to-mouth, Roberta instead stood up and stepped away from Ken, leaving him panting and wheezing on the ground.

She shook her head at him. 'You're pathetic, do you

know that? Flopping around on the ground like a greasy fish pulled from its pond. And that's all you are to the Old One: nothing but a lowly bottom feeder of a lifeform. But for me, it doesn't have to be that way. With Mother Sibbett to guide me, I can ascend into something else. Something more.'

As the girl rambled on, lost in the grandeur of her own speech, Ken could finally feel the pounding of his heart—and the pain that accompanied it—slowly start to subside. His breathing was still short and sharp; however, he felt his control over that return as well.

He began to clench and unclench his tingling hands, grasping at the grass and leaves below him, concentrating on the movements in an attempt to ignore, as much as he could, the wild woman who was jabbering away above him.

If he could get his breathing under control, then perhaps he had a chance. Ken wasn't sure if he was suffering from a severe panic attack or mild heart attack—he suspected the latter—but either way, he had to force his body and heart to slow down. Gradually, his breathing became more regular.

In through the nose, out through the mouth.

'We are so ignorant to the truth of life,' Roberta went on. 'Little mites scurrying around in our own plane of existence, confident we have everything figured out. But we have no idea how things really are, and know nothing of the other places that exist, bordering our own. Touching it. And sometimes, the other side breaks through.'

Ken squeezed his hands again and managed to move his left one from side to side a little. Roberta was now looking up to the heavens with arms held aloft.

'The lines of existence here—between our world and the other—have blurred, allowing the Old One to come through.'

Roberta went on and Ken's movement became easier, if only slightly. His left palm rolled across an object in the grass, settling on something thick, cold, and coarse. He recognised it to be a branch of some kind, the end poking out from beneath his form. He quickly realised that this was the object he had landed on, and it was perhaps a nub or broken offshoot that had dug into his back and caused the sharp pain after his fall.

Ken wrapped his fingers around it, but the girth of the sturdy branch was too wide to allow his fingertips to meet.

Though it was stuck beneath him and—given Ken's weakened state—not easily accessible, he hoped it would make a formidable weapon if he could summon the strength to stand and swing it. Perhaps falling on this spot, right onto the branch, had been his first piece of good luck since setting foot in the Black Forest.

'And Mother Sibbett was chosen as the grotesque God's emissary. She, in turn, has taken me to her bosom, allowing me to learn from her. To indulge in sacred knowledge. And what I have learned already, dear Ken, has opened my mind. Unlocked it to the truth.'

'It's turned you mad,' Ken told her in a wheezing voice.

'No,' Roberta answered, shaking her head. 'What you see as madness is merely something beyond your comprehension.'

'You're a monster.'

She let out a humourless laugh in response. 'Oh, you have no idea. The things I did to poor James would sicken you. But those acts, fun as they were, also allowed me to grow, to become more than I ever could have been before.'

Ken slowly rotated his body and rolled to the right, lifting his back off of the log beneath him. Pain flared, but he managed to keep his movements subtle enough that

Roberta didn't notice. His hand found purchase on the makeshift club, and he gently slid it out from underneath him. Roberta was still looking to the stars, as if she could see something wondrous that Ken wasn't privy to, giving him the opportunity to act.

But the sound of the log sliding across the ground, against leaves and grass, alerted her, and she looked down on him.

'And Mother Sibbett has something special planned for you, too, Ken,' she went on, seemingly ignoring what he was doing. 'You could yet have a purpose. You don't need to join Tony and James in their eternal fate. All you need to do is to give yourself over to Mother willingly.'

'Never!' Ken shot back, pulling the branch free completely. He held it tightly in both hands like a sword, pointing it out away from him to hopefully fend her off.

Ken had hoped to be able to get up and take a swing without Roberta expecting it, but that plan had been ruined the second she had looked down. The element of surprise was now lost.

However, Roberta didn't seem fazed by the sight of him with a weapon in hand. And in truth, why should she be? He was still stuck on his back, weak as a puppy, and Roberta was up on her feet.

'You think that little twig will do you any good?' Roberta asked, cocking her head to the side. As she did, a blister on the side of her neck burst. Clear liquid spurted free. The black spot beneath the punctured skin rotated and settled on Ken, and only then did he realise it was a pupil that had previously been trapped beneath the surface. Now he could see it was part of the bulbous flesh of an eye, looking more like a fish-eye than anything human.

Roberta then moved back, actually giving Ken more

space, as if goading him to act. Not looking a gift-horse in the mouth, Ken used the opportunity to force himself up to his feet. It took effort—causing him to run short of breath again—and he needed to use the branch as a crutch to keep his balance, but he finally made it to a vertical base. His legs felt like jelly, and it took him a few moments to be able to hold his own weight and then draw back the club, readying himself like a batter waiting for a pitch. The weapon in his grasp felt like it weighed a ton, and Ken suddenly doubted his ability to be able to swing it hard enough or true enough to do any significant damage.

Roberta chuckled, seemingly amused. 'Oh, this should be good. Come on, Ken, you're on death's door. Do you really think you can hurt me?'

'I can try,' he said through gritted teeth. 'And if you don't fuck off and leave me alone, I'll show you just how much damage I can do.'

Roberta put her hands behind her back and started to pace forward, bouncing up and down with each step, exaggerating each movement.

'Tell you what,' she said. 'I'll give you a free swing. Do your worst.'

Ken backed up, trying to keep distance between them, but stumbled a little as he did. Roberta, however, kept coming, moving slowly herself, but gaining ground easily. Ken knew he couldn't outrun her. If he had any hope of getting away, then he would need to take this opportunity.

But this was Roberta.

It may be true that she was a monster now—quite literally—but was it possible the real woman was still there somewhere, trapped beneath the surface? Still able to see and feel everything that was happening to her. Could he really try to hurt a woman that, over the past few years, he had come to call a friend?

'Can't do it, can you,' she said, either reading his thoughts or seeing the doubt that must have been written all over his face.

'I can,' he snapped back, trying to convince himself more than her.

She walked right up to him. 'Then do it. If you can't, just drop the stick and quit fucking around. We've got some-where to be... and someone to meet.'

Ken clenched his weapon tighter. Despite his reserva-tions, he knew there wasn't really a choice to make. If he didn't try to fend Roberta off, he was a dead man. And he knew the end waiting for him would not be pleasant. It would be horrific and painful.

That thought, as much as anything, spurred him to act.

Ken swung, throwing every ounce of strength he had behind the movement—starting low and bringing the club upwards in an arc as hard as he could.

Ken felt the vibrations of the impact run from the weapon and up through his arms, stinging his palms, threat-ening to shake the branch free from his grip. A sickening crack rang out when the wood connected with Roberta's chin, and her head snapped back. A jet of black blood spat up into the air from her mouth, and Roberta fell backwards, sprawling out across the ground, staying motionless after she had settled.

Ken didn't need any further invitation to escape. He turned and moved away as quickly as he could, again using the branch—this time as a crutch to help him walk. Running was out of the question, his heart just would not take it, but he tried to push himself.

However, the ground he had made up before that sound stopped him was minimal, managing only a few metres.

The noise he heard was a groan, coming from Roberta. But it was not one of pain or grogginess. Ken turned back to see the floored woman begin to move. Her arms rose above her head as her back arched. The moaning continued, but to Ken it actually sounded... pleasurable. Then her body began to convulse, and she let out screams of pleasure and her fingers grasped at the ground, pulling out clumps of dirt.

Ken couldn't believe what he was seeing. Hitting her with the branch had, bizarrely, driven her to some kind of climax.

Eventually, Roberta calmed down, and her convulsions eased off. Whatever pleasure she had been feeling had peaked and was now falling away. Then she suddenly sat up in one fluid motion. Her jaw hung loosely at a horrible angle, wobbling after her quick movement.

And yet again, the mad woman began to laugh. It was a sound Ken was utterly sick of by now, but this time it was different. The laughter that bellowed from Roberta now seemed to take her over completely, and she threw her head back as her whole body shook.

Ken turned away and again tried to escape, but he heard the cackling witch get to her feet as well. She began to run after him.

And Ken knew he was fucked.

35

KEN SHOULD HAVE JUST DROPPED to the ground and let Roberta take him.

He'd tried to break into a run, an instinctual reaction to being chased. But his heart exploded in pain again, and he stopped short, grasping at his chest.

He then felt a great force hit him from behind and shove him to the ground, face first. Ken could barely even summon the strength to lift his head out of the smothering dirt and grass.

The agony that fired out of his heart with every beat was like an electric shock. He wanted to cry out in pain, but he could instead only create a pitiful mewling sound. He couldn't even roll himself over to face the terror that plagued him, still cackling that maddening laugh.

He then felt hands take hold of him by the arms and roll him to his front. Roberta stood above him, and he looked up at her naked, sickening form. Those black spots beneath the surface of the skin that he now knew to be alien-like eyes all focused on him. Others had broken free after warts that previously enclosed them had also popped.

Roberta then slowly lifted her hands to her twisted jaw and took hold. In a quick motion, she snapped it back into place—a dull crack sounding as she did. A long, low groan escaped her. Then she turned her attention back to Ken and looked down at him.

Without a word he watched as she again brought up a hand, only this time Roberta took hold of a greasy length of tangled hair. She yanked, and Ken winced as he heard the clump of threads pull free from her flesh. Then she bent down and used the rope-like hair to bind his wrists together in an inventive, if gross, restraint.

The next words she spoke were garbled, thanks to her jaw, but still understandable. 'Time to go.'

Roberta took hold of Ken's ankles, one in each hand, and began walking, dragging Ken along behind her. The restraints on his wrists weren't even needed, as by trying to run again he'd exacerbated the attack he was having, causing it to flare up considerably and debilitating him completely. His only feeling was of pain, both from his heart, and from the rocks that dug into him as Ken was pulled along the ground.

He could only look up at the stars above as dirt and old, dead leaves clung to him, caking his clothes and hair in filth. Helpless to fight back and save himself, Ken knew there was now only one way it was all going to end. And, perhaps, it was what he deserved after all.

It didn't take him long to pass out, his body ravaged with exhaustion and pain.

But Roberta kept going, dragging her victim for over two hours. To the original site of the village.

Where Mother Sibbett awaited.

36

THE LIGHT SNAPPING and crackling sound was the first thing Ken noticed. Consciousness was slow in regaining its hold on him, and he could smell something smokey, everything happening before he'd opened his eyes.

His thoughts aligned and Ken soon remembered the intense pain he had been enduring before he'd passed out. And he remembered being dragged along behind Roberta; however, he was no longer moving, though his hands were now unbound. He lay on his back on rough terrain, but knew that he was not alone, hearing the murmurs of things close to him. He could also detect pained sobs from farther away.

His body still ached with pain, especially his chest, but the urgency and fierceness of that pain had eased, indicating the attack had passed. But its after-effects still lingered on.

Damn it, why couldn't I have died?

Ken knew dying would have been preferable to whatever fate awaited him when he eventually opened his eyes, something he was reluctant to do.

Eventually, however, he had to.

Ken's vision was initially blurred as flickering light penetrated his watering eyes. After blinking to clear his sight, he noted that the source of this light was coming from straight ahead. A tall bonfire engulfed in yellow and red flame licked at the night sky.

And things moved within the flames, between the glowing waste material of logs, branches, and wooden doors that all fuelled the fire. Ken could see that there were people in amongst the inferno—their bodies black and bubbling.

Looking around, he also became aware that he was lying on the ground in the centre of a small village that was similar to the last one he'd stood in. He saw the same circular well and, behind the bonfire, could even see that damned stone church.

While Ken could see that the low, pained sobs were coming from the poor souls trapped within the bonfire, the hungry murmurs he heard were emanating from the other things that were gathered.

The village folk Ken had previously encountered—with their twisted faces and drab, dark clothing—surrounded both him and the fire, though they gave a respectful and healthy distance to the flames. They watched the bodies writhe within and took great glee at the suffering, but with every pop and crackle they winced and jumped, as if scared of the purging element.

Roberta sat next to Ken, cross-legged, facing off towards the burning that had so delighted all of the other souls present. He could smell her, but only just, as the odour of burning meat and smoke that came from the great fire was almost all-encompassing.

When he studied the girl, Ken could see more of those

horrible, clustered fish-eyes on her skin, and they rolled to face him. A smirk drew over her face. Ken wasn't sure how long he had been unconscious, but Roberta had changed even more during that time, now little more than a skeleton with a thin layer of mottled skin stretched tightly over her frame. Only the barnacle-like clusters of eyes broke up the boney expanse of dry, darkened flesh.

'Awake I see,' she whispered to him without taking her eyes off the fire. Her voice sounded much clearer now, her jaw working with no issues. Though it still had that hoarse, raspy quality to it.

'You can see out of those things?' Ken whispered back, referring to the fleshy bulbs that littered her body. He kept his voice low, not wanting to draw the attention of any of the others.

'I see everything,' she told him.

Ken didn't attempt to move. There was no point. So he turned his attention back to the fire, seeing the victims within still moving. He had no idea how long the fire had been going, but surely the life of those unfortunates should have been extinguished by now. Ken slowly raised a hand and pointed to them. 'Will they ever die?'

'They are already dead,' Roberta answered. 'But they will never stop feeling what is happening to them.'

'Who are they? Why aren't they out here with the rest of you?'

'They don't deserve a place out here with us. They are the unbelievers. People of this village who shunned Mother's teachings. Resisted. So this is their penance. And there are others, too. Unfortunates who have wandered here and been taken throughout the years. All as sustenance and sacrifice to the Old One.'

Ken's mind ran back to the last time he had been in the village, to the well that had been packed with bodies. He didn't need to be told they were the same people. 'So, they are just tortured for eternity now?'

Roberta nodded. 'That's right. Such is the fate of the unworthy. You know,' she deftly lowered her head to him, 'If you look closely, you may recognise some of them.'

It was her turn to point now. 'Towards the tip of the flames, right at the top. Do you see it?'

Ken squinted in an attempt to see more clearly. He could make out something impaled on a branch at the very head of the bonfire. It was being held just out of the main body of the inferno, but was still being cooked by the heat and the jumping flames. Something on that object was moving. It took Ken a moment to realise that it was, in fact, a black and blistered human head. The jaw was opening and closing in a silent scream. But at this distance, Ken could make out no more, which he took as a blessing.

'Who is it?' he asked.

'Tony,' Roberta answered, as if it was the most obvious thing in the world. Ken felt his blood turn to ice despite all of the heat of the raging fire. 'That is his existence now. Mother Sibbett twisted off his head after she took him. But not before laying claim to his essence.'

If Ken had felt guilty at the fates of his friends before, now that he could see and understand the full nature of their suffering, his shame only intensified. Ken hadn't just cost these people their lives; he'd given them everlasting damnation.

'Jesus,' he uttered.

Roberta scoffed. 'Well, he can't help you here. And neither can his dad. Not that his father even existed, of course. The only God you need to worry about is the Old

One. Because, if you don't please it, you can look forward to the same kind of existence Tony and James now share.'

Ken took a moment to answer back, still struggling with what he was seeing. 'And what could this Old One possibly want with me?' he asked, feeling tears well up in his eyes, unable to turn his attention away from the head of Tony at the tip of the fire.

She shrugged. 'It knows you feel immense pain. An agony built up over many years. I think the Old One has taken an interest in that. Pain and agony help sustain it here, and we must give it what it needs.'

'I'll never be like you,' Ken said. 'I'd rather die.'

'And exist forever like that?' Roberta asked, again pointing to Tony.

Ken paused. The thought of willingly giving himself over to this entity—whatever it was—sickened him. But knowing he could share the same eternal pain Tony was now feeling terrified Ken to his core.

'Thought not,' Roberta said. 'Now, ready yourself. It's time. She is coming to take you.'

Ken wrinkled his brow, and he was about to ask Roberta who she was talking about, but saw that the witch was no longer looking at the fire, instead at the church beyond it. Both leaves of the door were now open, and from the blackness within something came out. A sight that made Ken's bladder release.

Like a spider emerging from a small hole, long and thin limbs poked out from the black. They pulled with it an elongated body covered with the same fleshy eyes as Roberta. The face of the wretched thing, as it rose up, was a horrific mess of features—some human, some not. The thing then pulled itself up to its fullest height, towering far above the head of the door it had just emerged from. Ken noticed something strapped to its sagging torso, but could not focus on what as the spindly, nightmarish form of Mother Sibbett strode over towards him, its thudding footsteps sending vibrations through the very ground beneath.

Excited sounds went up from the villagers, and Ken began to scream in manic terror.

37

'HELP ME!' Ken yelled to Roberta, praying there was a shred of humanity left in her. 'For the love of God, please help me!'

But Roberta didn't. Of course she didn't. There was truly no mercy or compassion left within that ruined body.

'Sorry, Ken,' she said as the giant beast stalked its way over, making sure to avoid the roaring fire. 'There is no surviving this. You're hers now. But you still have a choice to make. Remember that. It could save you, in a way.'

Ken tried to move, to wriggle himself away, but he could do little more than slither across the ground like a snake. Mother Sibbett, now impossibly large, planted her feet on either side of him and stood tall, looking down at his cowering form.

Ken kept up his screaming. At this close a distance, the sight of her was even more overwhelming to him. Those disgusting, roving fish-eyes all moved of their own accord, flitting around in different directions. Her dry skin pulsed and moved as if something was shifting beneath the surface.

And, to his horror, Ken could now plainly see what it was that had been strapped to her torso.

A man groaned, eyes rolling in his head as if he was barely conscious. His stomach was open, and the intestines had been pulled out, wrapping around the large frame behind, securing him to it. The man's legs and arms had been pulled into the flesh of the creature's chest, disappearing beneath the skin. Looking closely, Ken could see that the borders where skin met limb were slowly advancing all the time, sucking the unfortunate man inside of it very slowly. Even the man's head had begun to submerge, with the flesh lapping over the top of his skull.

It was James.

'Hi, lover,' Roberta called up to the suffering man, waving as she stood to her feet. 'Hope you are having fun with Mother!'

She laughed. The giant witch also made a sound—a high-pitched, shrieking titter—that, while not exactly human, Ken took for laughter as well. A large hand, ending in blackened claws, lowered down and gently patted Roberta on the head. It was the affection shown to a pet.

The sight before Ken made no sense on many levels. For one, it was disturbing to behold. But beyond that was the fact that he had seen this hag before, as a still image on the footage taken earlier. In it, though hidden behind a tree, she had been of normal height. And her features had not been as twisted as what he now gazed upon.

'This... this isn't possible,' Ken stammered. 'What happened to her? What *is* she?'

'An emissary,' Roberta said. 'As I told you. Through her, the Old One can make its will known.'

'But we saw her before. She wasn't—'

Roberta sniggered. 'Mother can appear to you in many different ways.'

Ken didn't have time to ask any more questions. Another hand lowered, this one coming straight for him. Ken squirmed backwards in panic, and managed to get up onto his elbows, but his feeble escape was cut short as the sharp fingers grabbed his right leg, the tips of the claws digging into the skin of his thigh and puncturing the flesh. He screamed as he was hoisted high up into the air, dangling upside down, level with James.

The groaning man didn't notice Ken hanging before him, however, his milky eyes instead lost in pain as the flesh of the torso slowly devoured him. Ken was then lifted higher up, to the terrifying face of the monster. Rank breath flowed over him as Ken stared into the massive yellow eyes that blinked ahead of him. Would this living nightmare devour him? Just drop him into a maw lined with sharp, crooked, teeth?

As it turned out, that was not her plan. Mother Sibbett instead turned and thundered back towards the church. A loud cheer went up from the village-folk. She rounded the fire, ducked down, and entered the church again, with Ken still struggling in her grasp.

38

JUST LIKE THE last time Ken had been inside of this infernal place, the church was once again home to those displayed bodies, again intertwined and sewn together in poses and acts of debauchery. He could see them writhe and move, backing away from the great giant that stomped her way down the central aisle.

Ken's head filled with blood as he was carried upside-down—helpless—by Mother Sibbett while she moved to the front of the church. Again, seated at the altar he was being carried towards, was that goat-headed figure he had seen before, still in the same cross-legged position with one arm out to the side. The horns that sprouted from the black fur of its crown rose up high, ending in sharp points. And from the female figure's wrinkled breasts—ones that hung low to the midsection—black liquid dripped free, pooling on the occult symbol on which it sat.

Ken had no idea what this horrific depiction was supposed to represent, but he was dropped directly in front of it. He hit the ground hard, and the air was driven out of his lungs. He could scarcely stop shaking and, even though he was still weak, sat upright. He then looked back to the towering nightmare that looked down on him. The monster's head was level with the roof rafters, where moving corpses with their insides on display were tied. The witch then, in what looked like an absentminded act, reached up a hand and grabbed the leg of one such captive. With a twist, the leg was pulled free, popping off like the leg of a cooked chicken, and dropped to the floor. The poor soul it belonged to—strapped with arms outstretched and tied to the horizontal crosspiece—whined in agony, but had no jaw to fully vocalise its pain. Ken couldn't even tell the gender of the undead person, given the torn and mangled state of its body.

Ken then looked through the thin, withered legs of Mother Sibbett, and he saw that the crowd from outside were filtering inside. At the head of the mass of people, of course, was Roberta, who continued down the aisle and stood beside Mother, like the obedient pet that she was.

'Why did she bring me here?' Ken asked, pointing up to Mother Sibbett, looking at her grinning face and awful, wild eyes. Scanning down her body further, Ken could make out her sickeningly thin frame, and the cluster of tumour-like eyes that covered it. He also noted a thicket of coarse, black hair that covered the sex of the monster and ran up to her belly. The very sight of Mother Sibbett disgusted Ken.

'To end it,' Roberta answered him. 'It's time, Ken. Time to do what she wills of you. Give yourself over.'

Ken tried to crab-walk backwards, but even this simple movement made his heart once again surge into overdrive, causing pain to spike with every beat. On top of that, he had only succeeded in moving maybe a foot before his head bounced off the soft, spongy stomach of the effigy behind. He looked up to see the bestial, dead face of the horned animal as it now angled its head to look down on him. The horizontal pupils that cut a black line through the dull yellow around them felt like they were staring into his very soul.

Ken's chest tightened, and his breathing became short and rasping. Regardless of the horrors around him, he knew that there was no way he was going to get out of this situation alive. Even if Mother Sibbett and her followers hadn't been present, the condition of his heart coupled with the lack of medical assistance made it a certainty that he was going to die in these woods. And soon.

Survival for him now was just not an option. But he had no time to dwell on that. The demons around him would not allow it. However, if he could not choose to save his own life, then perhaps he could instead decide how to end it.

Ken looked past the grinning face of the goat that hovered over him, up to its pointed horns.

Sharing the fate of Tony and James terrified him to an extent that threatened to loosen his bladder again. But, at the same time, willfully giving himself over to Mother Sibbett as Roberta had suggested would inevitably lead to something much worse.

However, if he instead took his own life, perhaps he could spare himself torturous pain and eternal damnation.

'And just how... do you expect me... to give myself to her?' Ken asked, his words slow and laboured, a struggle to get out.

'First,' Roberta replied with a smile that showed her blackened teeth and gums, 'You need to take on the blood of the Old One.'

'Is that what happened to you?'

Roberta nodded. 'When we first arrived here. It fell from a tree, dropped by Mother's will. The Great Blood flows through this forest, spreading the influence of Mother Sibbett and the Old One. Tony, too, was infected through the wound on his neck. As for James,' Roberta let a smile sneak across her lips, 'I was the one who made sure he was infected.' She then pointed to the goat-headed thing behind Ken. 'See that? It is our representation of the Old One.'

Ken looked back, still appalled by the creation, but surprised that this was the thing they worshipped. Especially given the twenty-foot monster that stood above them, which was a much more terrifying sight.

'*That* is the Old One?'

Roberta laughed. 'No. Only Mother has truly seen the Old One. But the rest of us are not strong enough to do so. Not yet. This is just our effigy, our fetish of it. But the blood still flows within that dead husk.'

She then nodded towards the dripping breasts. Ken's eyes widened in realisation.

'No! No fucking way!'

His former friend just laughed again, taking great glee at his sudden understanding. 'Oh yes. You need the blood inside of you, Ken. So take it.'

'That's sick.'

'It is,' she said. 'But that's the point. You need to unburden yourself of the restraints of what you have been taught. There is no right or wrong here. There is only the way of things. Now... drink.'

From above, Mother Sibbett bent at her knees, lowering her monstrous face down closer to him. Breath like rotting meat spilt over him as she waited for Ken—waited for him to willfully give himself over.

Silence descended over the gathered village-folk. All eyes in the church now rested on Ken.

There was no place for him to run, and even if there was, he didn't have the strength to try.

There was no way out.

So he slowly brought himself up to his knees, using the effigy of The Old One as support for his weakened body. Ken's face drew level to the awful breasts of the thing before him, and his left hand grabbed one of the sharp horns above to steady himself.

And to prepare himself.

Perhaps he did not have the energy to escape, but maybe he had strength enough for one last act. It would be a defiant one, but it would allow him to end things on his own terms.

Ken's hand squeezed around the horn. It felt strong and sturdy in his grip, which was what he'd hoped. Ken then moved his head closer to the long, purple nipple, hearing excited murmurs from the congregation behind him as he did.

Good, let them get excited.

All he was doing was keeping up a pretence.

He looked to the line across the throat of the effigy, where beast met human. The two parts were held together by a simple stitch of thin and frail-looking thread. Though Ken's energy felt almost depleted, he hoped he still had strength enough for what he had in mind.

And so, with every ounce of energy he had, Ken spun his body, ripping at the goat head and letting out a weak roar as he did. Thankfully, he heard the stitching tear and felt the head give way and detach from the body, which flopped to the floor by his side. Ken let himself fall back into it, with the prize still in hand.

A furious roar went up around the room, with Roberta letting out a screech of anger.

Ken, acting quickly, had already rotated the head that he held in his hands so that one of the prongs was aimed directly at back him.

The giant witch above him just watched, not even blinking as he stared back into her eyes, teeth clenched.

'Fuck you, bitch,' he said. Ken then closed his eyes and yanked the tip of the horn down to his exposed throat.

39

HE'D BRACED for the pain, fully expecting the piercing of his trachea to be an explosion of agony. But he needed to bear it, as Ken planned on yanking the makeshift spear around as hard as he could in order to rip open the wound as much as possible. Then there would be no turning back. Lastly, of course, he would have to endure the act of actually dying. But he was ready for all of that.

What he was not ready for, however, was what he actually felt... nothing. No stabbing pain, no tearing of the flesh, no puncturing of his throat. The sharp horn had not pierced his skin.

When Ken opened his eyes, he saw precisely why.

Large, claw-like fingers held the horned goat head between them, overpowering Ken, stopping him from completing his suicidal motion.

The animal's head was then quickly snatched from Ken's grasp and thrown back into the gathered village-folk who had packed the church.

'That was a mistake,' Roberta said, her mouth curled up into a snarl.

But Ken wasn't sure that was true. Even if he had to suffer unimaginable pain, he felt it preferable to submitting to the madness.

Though that mindset could change, of course.

Ken moved backwards, climbing over the decapitated body of the effigy behind him. That in itself was a struggle, and his heart continued to beat frantically. He couldn't escape, as there was nowhere to go. There was no secret door behind him that he could make use of. And even if there was, he didn't have the strength to make use of it. Crawling away from the giant and her followers, like a bug on the ground, was pushing Ken to his absolute limit. Roberta walked towards him, though the witch above seemed satisfied to hold her ground.

'There's nowhere to go, Ken,' she said, quickly catching up to him. She then raised a filthy foot and drove it down onto Ken's chest. An eruption of pain bloomed beneath her sole as it slammed into him and pinned him easily to the floor. 'So this defiance is pointless.'

'It's... done,' Ken said, wheezing. 'I won't... submit.'

Roberta bared her teeth and lifted her foot, ready to stamp it down again. Ken tensed, waiting for the blow, but Roberta stopped. The rage on her face melted away, and she turned her head towards Mother Sibbett. Roberta held the giant's gaze for a while, merely looking at the monster.

What is she doing? Ken thought, still expecting her to drive her foot down once again.

But instead, a smile crossed over Roberta's face and, eventually, she turned back to Ken. 'You're right, Mother,' she said.

Ken realised there was some kind of communication taking place that he wasn't party to.

'What's... going on?' he asked.

'Mother Sibbett has decided to give you another chance,' she told him.

'Fuck... you.'

'You might change your mind when you hear what she has to say. Thing is, Mother Sibbett knows why you are here. She knows what it is you're searching for more than anything else in the world. And she has the knowledge that you need to get the answers.'

'What... do you... mean?'

'You want to know what happens after we die? Well, she can answer that. She can show you what happened to Amy, Ken. She feels your guilt, your anguish, and it excites the Old One. It has been a long time since they've had someone so burdened with pain cross the threshold of the forest. So, if you agree, then you will get what you want. The Old One can make it happen. It can reunite you with Amy.'

'Bullshit!'

'No. It's true.'

'Amy is dead,' Ken said through clenched teeth. 'She has *nothing* to do with this place.'

Roberta paused, looking again at Mother Sibbett as more unspoken words were seemingly shared. She turned back to Ken.

'There is something you should know, Ken. Out there, in the world beyond the borders of the forest, things are different. Dead is dead. There is no afterlife outside of the influence of Old One, or those like it. So your Amy, dear Ken, is no more. Nothing. She doesn't exist.'

Ken tried to spit at Roberta in anger, but the effort was pathetic, and he did little more than send a trail of saliva down his own chin. The intent, however, was not lost on her.

'Don't get angry,' Roberta said with a small giggle. 'Hear me out. What I'm telling you is true. But the thing is, you are in a place outside of the restraints of your world. Death isn't the end here—or, at least, it doesn't have to be. Mother Sibbett and the Old One can offer you something. They can make it so that you can see your daughter again. You can live with her every day for eternity, seeing her smiling face. Every. Single. Day. Until the end of time.'

'Lies,' Ken responded, certain he was being deceived.

'No,' Roberta insisted.

'But it won't be real.'

'That's the thing. It will *seem* real to you. Because you won't know any better. Your soul, or part of it, will think it's all real. So, in essence, it will be. You won't remember any of this: the forest, your dead friends, or this church. None of it. You will only know the reality that surrounds you.'

'It's a trick,' Ken said, but the certainty was gone.

What if it wasn't a trick? If what they offered was a possibility, then even if it wasn't the real Amy, wasn't that existence preferable to the alternatives: eternal torment or eternal nothingness?

How could he seriously choose one of those fates?

And the thought that his daughter had stepped into the infinite void of the second option was enough to shatter his mind as much as it broke his heart.

But what if he could forget all of that pain and anguish and guilt?

Real or not, to carry on in ignorance, to be able to see his daughter again would indeed be heaven compared to the hell of this life since her death.

'And what's... in it for you?' Ken asked. The pain in his chest was still agonising, but he needed to get the words out. He needed to know. 'Why would you do that? Wouldn't that stop you from getting what you want? My pain and suffering.'

Roberta shook her head. 'No, it wouldn't. In fact, it would give Mother and the Old One *exactly* what they want. Let them take your pain away from you. I promise, they can make it real for you. And you will see your daughter, just as you remember her. And you will never know what happened here. We aren't lying to you, Ken.'

She then knelt down beside him and held up her wrist level with Ken's head. With her other hand, she drew a sharp nail across her skin and veins, cutting away the flesh in one swipe. Black liquid bubbled free and flowed down her arm. Roberta then moved her wrist closer to him, and he understood what he was to do.

'Drink,' she told him. 'And see Amy again.'

A voice screamed in the back of his mind, telling him to resist. It was the same voice that had warned him earlier when he'd seen the apparition of Amy in the forest. But the promise of what *could* be was powerful, just as it had been when he had seen Amy. Ken now had a similar choice to make, in a way, and it was one he had gotten wrong before. Back then, he should have just turned away from the sight of her, knowing it wasn't real, and run. And now, somewhere in his consciousness, he knew the things he was being promised likely came with a price. Or they were outright lies.

So the choice should have been obvious.

But, that was the thing with unresolved grief and guilt—it could override common sense and logic, as Ken was all too aware. So deep was his river of pain that he would do whatever it took to get out and stop from drowning. However small the chance, the offer before Ken could potentially give him everything he'd ever wanted since the day his daughter died.

Absolution.

And if it was a trick, then perhaps he would get what he really deserved.

But if not... well, the promise of that was too strong of a pull.

Tears rolled down Ken's cheeks, and he clamped his mouth over the proffered wrist. He sucked, gobbling down mouthfuls of the foul, sour-tasting blood.

'Good,' Roberta said with a large, sinister smile. 'Good.'

40

KEN WASN'T sure how much of the so-called 'Great Blood' now sloshed around in his belly. It was enough to make him feel nauseous, certainly, but he didn't know how much more he could stomach. Thankfully, Roberta eventually withdrew her wrist, drawing to a close the grotesque feeding.

'Well done,' she said. 'You've made the right decision.'

'Were you telling the truth?' Ken asked, braced for an answer he did not want, but one he fully expected. 'About seeing Amy again?'

Roberta paused before replying, but only for a moment. However, it was long enough to feel like an eternity to Ken. 'No,' she eventually said. 'You *will* see her. Every day. Like we promised. And you will have no memory of any of this. But...'

She trailed off, smiling.

'But what?' Ken asked, knowing that something was coming to sour the deal. He'd been so fucking stupid.

'Well, the blood is inside of you now, Ken. The blood of the Old One. So when you die, your soul will live on in a state desired by the one we serve. That is where you will see

Amy again, in an existence forged by its will. However, that will only happen in death. So there is the small matter of ending your life to take care of.' She chuckled. Excited murmurs grew from those present inside of this hellish church.

Ken understood now. This was the trade-off. This was where these demonic creatures would take their payment.

And so it was.

Ken was mutilated and torn asunder.

First, the giant form of Mother Sibbett reached a gnarled and clawed hand down towards him, driving the nail of one huge finger through his shoulder. He screamed, but that was just the start—only a way to keep him in place.

Led by Roberta, the village-folk inside of the church all descended onto him as their Mother watched on from above. Scores of hands grasped at Ken and bodies piled on top of him. The sodomy was both painful and humiliating, but it was only a way to ease him into the coming torture.

He was abused and defiled, and the skin was torn off his writhing body. The grasping hands that fought over him became more violent: entrails and intestines were pulled free and gorged on by the demons that were killing him.

Ken was unable to scream anymore—with no jaw or vocal cords—as he endured unimaginable agony.

It was Roberta he saw last before death claimed him. She lowered her disgusting head over him and smiled. It was a sweet smile, at least, as much as her ruined face would allow, and she waved.

The price of eternal happiness had indeed been high. The pain was excruciating and almost beyond comprehension. And the humiliation at how his body was being used was perhaps even worse.

But as much as it felt like the slow death would never

end, Ken knew—somewhere in the back of his mind—that it would.

And it finally did.

His light slowly extinguished, and he could focus only on Roberta as his vision faded to black.

It was over now. He could look forward to continuing on in blissful ignorance with the person he loved most in this world. The price, he knew, had been worth it.

A thought entered Ken's mind before it ceased its function: *did Tony and James have to submit the same way? Or did they suffer this kind of end regardless?*

He couldn't think it through any further, however, as his brain activity ceased. The words spoken to him by Roberta went unheard.

'Go now, Ken,' she had said. 'Go see your little girl.'

41

'DADDY, WAKE UP!'

It was Amy's voice. His daughter.

Ken stirred, rousing himself from a deep sleep. A gentle breeze from an open window felt good against his cheek. But he didn't feel ready to wake up just yet. Even through his closed eyelids, he could detect daylight flooding into the room. Small hands began to shake him.

When Ken eventually opened his eyes and looked up, Amy was staring down at him with a big smile. She was still in her pajamas, and her hair was a glorious mop of wild blonde frizz.

'Wake up,' she said again. 'Mom's gone to work already.'

Memory began to seep back to him, replacing a dream he couldn't remember. And then his eyes opened even wider.

Today was the big day. An important day. One he couldn't afford to mess up. Ken jumped out of bed, now a bundle of nerves, knowing today was not going to be anything less than perfect.

He'd have to take Amy with him now, which was a

change to the plan, and not ideal. But he would still make it work.

'Can we play a game, Daddy? You promised to play hide and seek with me today.'

'Not now, Amy,' Ken replied. 'I have an important meeting to get ready for.'

'But you said we could play,' she whined, stamping her little foot. Amy wasn't the type of child to throw a tantrum over nothing, and the smile on her face as she stomped indicated she was less than serious. But Ken had no time for games, and he could do without the distraction. He needed to focus.

'No!' he snapped, raising his voice. 'I don't have time to play with you. Now get ready.'

Ken saw the look of shock appear on her face. He felt bad, but made a mental note to make it up to her. They could play later, after his meeting.

There would always be time later.

Right now, though, he had more important things to worry about.

He spent the rest of the morning getting himself and Amy ready, running through the meeting in his head, trying to visualise how it would go and mentally prepare himself.

And then they set off. A traffic delay ruined his plan of being early, and so after parking in town he set off running, desperate to make up the time.

While en route, he phoned the agent to explain the situation.

'Daddy, wait,' he heard Amy say as they weaved between people. 'I can't keep up.'

'Yes, you can,' he told her, just as the agent answered the call. Ken explained his predicament and, thankfully, the man on the other end of the line understood. Even told him not to worry about it.

Then Ken heard something. A grunt from his daughter. Spinning his head, he saw her sprawled out on the road. Then he saw the truck. He looked at her.

Amy looked back.

Her eyes were so wide. So full of horror and fear. At that moment, the poor child understood something a girl of her age should never have to.

She understood what was going to happen to her.

Ken could do nothing, and the truck couldn't stop in time.

After the impact, while people around him shouted and panicked, Ken held her lifeless body. He screamed and screamed and screamed, loud and long enough for his voice to eventually give out. Ken thought he might actually die from the heartbreak.

His girl. His little girl. His Amy.

The rest of the day was a living nightmare of hellish guilt and suffering. He couldn't get the picture of her inno-cent face out of his mind, with that look of terrible under-standing drawing over her.

Ken lay on the sofa that night, nursing a picture of his daughter as he cried. He didn't remember falling asleep.

'DADDY, WAKE UP!'

It was Amy's voice. His daughter.

Small hands shook him. When Ken opened his eyes, he could see her staring down with a big smile. Realisation hit. Today was the day. An important day. One he had to be ready for.

'Can we play a game, Daddy? You promised to play hide and seek with me.'

'Not now, I have an important meeting to get ready for.'

'But you said we could play.'

'No! I don't have time to play with you today. Now get ready.'

They left. A build-up of traffic caused Ken to arrive in town late. They ran down the street. Ken phoned the agent to apologise. A grunt caught his attention.

Amy was in the road.

The truck. The screech. The look on her face. His life collapsing in an instant. His heart breaking in an explosion of pain beyond what he thought possible.

The rest of the day was a living hell. That night, Ken clutched a picture of her and cried.

He did not remember falling asleep.

∼

'DADDY, WAKE UP!'

It was Amy's voice. His daughter...

∼

THE END

THE DEMONIC

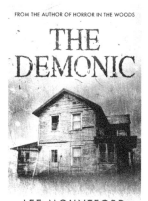

FROM THE AUTHOR OF HORROR IN THE WOODS

THE DEMONIC

LEE MOUNTFORD

Read more Supernatural Horror from Lee Mountford

Separate stories. The same, terrifying universe.

Years ago Danni Morgan ran away from her childhood home and vowed never to go back. It was a place of fear, pain and misery at the hands of an abusive father.

But now Danni's father is dead and she is forced to break her vow and return home—to lay his body to rest and face up to the ghosts of her past.

But Danni is about to realise that some ghosts are more real than others. And something beyond her understanding is waiting for her there, lurking in the shadows. An evil that intends to kill her family and claim her very soul.

Experience supernatural horror in the vein of THE

CONJURING, INSIDIOUS and the legendary GHOST-WATCH. THE DEMONIC will get under your skin, send chills down your spine and have you sleeping with the lights on!

Buy The Demonic now...

THE MARK

Read more Supernatural Horror from Lee Mountford

Separate stories. The same, terrifying universe.

Kirsty Thompson is no stranger to trauma. But when a vicious attack leaves her drugged and disoriented, she never expected to wake up to a permanent scar. She starts having demonic visions, all linked to the ancient symbol carved deep into her back...

With the help of her best friend Amanda, Kirsty discovers that the mark originates from The Devil's Bible and forges a connection between her and a terrifying creature. As they track the man who assaulted her to a satanic cult, the beast hunts them from the shadows. Can Kirsty escape the devil worshippers and her bond with the heinous creature to save herself from eternal damnation?

The Mark is a terrifying standalone horror novel. If you like mysterious depraved forces, tales of the occult, and stories that will have you looking under the bed, then you'll love this gripping tale!

Buy The Mark now...

HAUNTED: PERRON MANOR

A TERRIFYING HAUNTED HOUSE NOVEL.

Haunted: Perron Manor
Book 1 in the Haunted Series.
Sisters Sarah and Chloe inherit a house they could never have previously dreamed of owning. It seems too good to be true.

Shortly after they move in, however, the siblings start to notice strange things: horrible smells, sudden drops in temperature, as well as unexplainable sounds and feelings of being watched.

All of that is compounded when they find a study upstairs, filled with occult items and a strange book written in Latin.

Their experiences grow more frequent and more terrifying, building towards a heart-stopping climax where the sisters come face to face with the evil behind Perron Manor. Will they survive and save their very souls?

Buy Haunted: Perron Manor now.

THE EXTREME HORROR SERIES

Three stomach-churning horror novels in one volume.

Horror in the Woods – A group of friends are lost and hunted in the woods, pursued by a family of cannibals who are hungry for human flesh. Buy Horror in the Woods now.

Tormented – Insidious experiments are taking place at Arlington Asylum, and the helpless inmates are the test subjects. Buy Tormented now.

The Netherwell Horror – Looking for her brother after a troubling message, a journalist ends up in the strange fishing town of Netherwell Bay. There, she uncovers a plot by a sinister cult to bring about the end of days. Buy The Netherwell Horror now.

The Extreme Horror Collection collects the preceding novels in one volume. Buy it now, and strap in for three sickening tales that push the boundaries of horror.

The Extreme Horror Collection

THE BLACK FOREST

Sign up to my mailing list for a free horror book...

Enjoy *Forest of the Damned?*

Find out exactly what happened in that cursed forest all those years ago, and relive some of the most grisly events in its history.

The horrifying truth surrounding Mother Sibbett is revealed in *The Black Forest*, a prequel to *Forest of the Damned*. Sign up to my mailing list and get *The Nightmare Collection* free, which contains this prequel story.

www.leemountford.com

ABOUT THE AUTHOR

Lee Mountford is a horror author from the North-East of England. His first book, Horror in the Woods, was published in May 2017 to fantastic reviews, and his follow-up book, The Demonic, achieved Best Seller status in both Occult Horror and British Horror categories on Amazon.

He is a lifelong horror fan, much to the dismay of his amazing wife, Michelle, and his work is available in ebook, print and audiobook formats.

In August 2017 he and his wife welcomed their first daughter, Ella, into the world. In May 2019, their second daughter, Sophie, came along. Michelle is hoping the girls don't inherit their father's love of horror, but Lee has other ideas...

For more information
www.leemountford.com
leemountford01@googlemail.com

ACKNOWLEDGMENTS

Thanks first and foremost to my editor, Josiah Davis (http://www.jdbookservices.com), for such an amazing job.

The cover was supplied by Debbie at The Cover Collection (http://www.thecovercollection.com). I cannot recommend their work enough.

Thanks as well to fellow author—and guru extraordinaire—Iain Rob Wright for all of his fantastic advice and guidance. If you don't know who Iain is, remedy that now: http://www.iainrobwright.com. An amazing author with a brilliant body of work.

And the last thank you, as always, is the most important—to my amazing family. My wife, Michelle, and my daughters, Ella and Sophie—thank you for everything. You three are my world.

Made in the USA
Coppell, TX
27 October 2021